Eli's Rock

- a love story -

Cal & Claudia

Merry Christmas

with all my love.

Additional novels by Peter Randolph Keim

TA Buck Western Sagas
Reckoning on Blood River
Erastus: Long Trail til Sundown
Renegade Guns of Pomo Point
Stoney Bray: Last Sheriff of Cripple Creek

Kate Kingshott Western Novels
Goose Lake Rustlers

Jesse Crater Mysteries
Deep Threat: Murphys Gold
Hidden Threat: Ghost Boy
Sudden Threat: Reunion

Eli's Rock

- a love story -

by

Peter Randolph Keim

KeimRanchBooks

First Printing: 2011

Cover design: P. Randolph Keim
Editor: Gini Holcomb

Printed in the United States of America.

For Riley

Best of Breed
Our Little Buddy
Always a heart thought away

One

As she had all their married life, Ellie Ragsdale remained a wonderfully predictable constant. Beautiful in all the right ways. A butterfly. Modest, smart, faithful. Happy about the little things.

Like warm slippers.

The long, beaten path behind the barn to the river, bumped along slower than usual. *Age*, she'd say.

Ellie flowed like satin down the slope. So graceful. Ducked a bough. Looked her typical farm-wife self in her signature, homemade ankle length dress, apron. A rain bonnet tied in a bow beneath her chin - something delightful from 1860 perhaps. Hers was a covered wagon soul. She slowly lowered herself against the tree, melting into the fir tree's bark. Worn smooth from years of her frequent visits.

Her relaxed sigh in concert with the setting sun behind.

Eli Ragsdale, doting, grateful husband, arrived right behind. Stood above her, stiff arm leaning against the same fir. Always cheerful. Adored his wife. Marveled at her. Drank in her sweet smell.

Eli had shrunk some over the years. Wasn't tall to begin with. Ached often. Never complained. Neck hurt, knees throbbed. Droopy eyes studied a silvery shadow fighting the slow current.

A salmon?

Leaves, some yellow, some red, drifted by. It was fall. Transition months before winter. Still warm. Some drizzle. Wind.

Fir worked like an umbrella.

Couple worked their precious farm every day. Just not as rigorous. Been a long day. Eli pressed against the tree leveraging his way down into the needles and soft dirt next to Ellie. Bad hip kept him from simply sitting. He envied Ellie's ability to sit, squat, bend. Tie her shoes.

Pick up a *lucky* penny.

Eli dropped things. Sometimes deliberately. Left them. Knew Ellie picked them up without comment. He loved that. Loved her. Loved her butt when she bent.

Knew she loved *his* butt. Sagged some.

He leaned against her. Soft. Warm. He hummed.

She hummed.

As usual they met noses. Foreheads. Just what they did.

Usually didn't talk forehead to forehead. Eli swore he could *feel* her thoughts.

She smelled wonderful. Kind of a sweet, soapy smell. Same as always.

He smiled with his hum. She, too.

Eli settled his weathered hand over hers. Back of his hand was baby ass soft. Wrinkled. Veins like roots at the surface. Palm tough like horse hide.

"Another fine day, El. We got it done."

She purred a quiet *yes*. Pulled her head away from his. Now resting on the fir and Eli's shoulder.

"Baling is done for the year. I like that."

She hummed agreement.

"Frank and his boys here Wednesday to pick up the bales."

"Put our share in the barn?" Ellie asked turning more towards him.

Her breath like vanilla.

"They will."

"Can always count on Frank."

"We can." Eli said leaning towards the water for that salmon shadow.

"How many more, Eli?"

He sighed. Read her mind. "Couple."

"Said that five years ago."

"That's a fact."

"Mean it this time?"

"I do. Tired, El. Got good folks all around us. Strong. Young. Real good equipment. Field's never yielded more. Soil's still good, too."

"Field's had a good farmer."

"That's a fact." Eli smiled. Squeezed her hand. "Getting a chill. Walk?"

She nodded.

Trips to the river were a daily ritual. How long they stayed had diminished. Earth a bit firmer. Colder.

Ups and downs much more difficult.

They struggled up. Ellie first to help him.

That hip thing.

He leaned in for a kiss. Got cut off. She took his face in both her cupped hands. Soapy smell ran up his nostrils. Made him quiver.

"You have a cut on your cheek, Eli."

He felt his cheek. Looked at his finger. Mulled some. "Fence."

"How's that?"

"Buckshot stumbled across in front of me. We got tangled. I tripped. Caught myself on a fence post, but not before my face bumped the barbed wire. Didn't bleed much."

"Hurt?"

"Some. Stung."

"Where is that poor old dog?" Ellie asked turning a three-sixty along the river's bank.

"Left him sleeping by the barn. He knows where we are. Might not be able to see anymore, but his nose still works. 'Sides, been walking with us here every day since he was a pup. Fact is, he's getting too danged old to walk this far. Surprised he tries."

"Us, too." Ellie chuckled.

"Yep. Slow, but doable."

"Only 'bout a quarter mile. We're older'n that old cattle dog." Ellie said.

"That's a fact, Ellie."

Two

They found Buckshot at the top of the slope before the main crop field. Old Blue Heeler draped atop a bale of alfalfa. Paws crossed under his chin. Blue right eye wide open in a field of black. Other closed in a field of blue-gray.

They stopped to pet his coarse fur, mottled with various shaped patches of tan and black. One white one on each front shoulder.

Eye rolled shut to meet their touch.

Ellie hummed.

Buckshot the same.

Times he purred like a cat.

From where he stood, Eli looked about inspecting the firm, green bales of alfalfa dotting their acreage far up the slopes west and along the river north. Pulled a piece, stuck it in his mouth. Chewed it some.

"Well?" Ellie asked, still stroking Buckshot's hind quarters.

"Chews good." Eli said.

"Moisture?"

" 'Bout seventeen, maybe eighteen percent." He said pulling the hay from his mouth.

"Good." She said.

"That's a fact."

Like his *spot* on the window bench, the couch or the bed, any reachable cushion, Buckshot liked a little elevation. Liked perusing. They left him sleeping on the bale. He'd follow to the house when good and ready. Usually after sundown. There was still some light. Sometimes a little later if the field mice were running. It was fascinating to watch the nearly blind dog *listen* to the mice run. Head cocked. Turning to follow the scuttling tiny rodents.

Tip of his tail twitching.

Eli chuckled looking over his shoulder back at Buckshot. Knew one day that bale was as far as he and Ellie might make it.

Knew too, one day be no old dog sleeping there.

"Hungry?" Eli asked.

"You cooking?"

" 'Spose I could."

"Since when?" Ellie smirked.

"Or you can." He sighed.

"Take me out." Wasn't a question.

"I can." Where to?" Almost rhetorical. He knew the answer.

"Micki and Roy's okay with you?"

Feigning surprise, Eli clutched his heart. Stumbled back. Grabbed her arm. *"Reeeeally?"*

Going out to dinner was now more an adventure than ever. Ellie could no longer drive and Eli shouldn't, but did. Their children, three very grown adults who hadn't spoken to one another in years, threatened to take Eli's keys and truck. He stood firm.

"Our last vestige of independence and you wanna take it." He'd argue.

Ellie loved Mexican food. Not the hot stuff. Just the pure garden fresh taste of a chile relleno stuffed with a mild queso blanco in a not-too-hot verde sauce. Along with beans and rice. Ellie need never eat again. Micki and Roy's catered to her every need. She'd been a good and steady customer for twenty-two years. Ellie herself was a fine cook of many Mexican dishes. Years past she often served a full Mexican dinner to guests – even to Micki and Roy.

Eli, far less discerning, was a chip and salsa hombre. A burrito or enchilada. Loved rellenos. Inevitably he'd order the same as Ellie, but *his* slathered in hot salsa.

Ellie shook her head. Smiled. Nodded. "Yes. Of course, *reeeeally*." She was on her way to change her long dress and apron to something more appropriate for a *hot date*, as Eli would put it..

Eli looked over his closet. Dresser drawers. Shrugged and pulled a clean hanky from the drawer.

"Ready. Meet you outside." He yelled.

"Thanks for changing out of those smelly coveralls." Ellie replied from the bathroom.

Halfway through the kitchen Eli skidded to a stop. Smiled. Tiptoed back to his closet.

As he changed, "You're welcome."

Three

Indigestion, the growling stomach kind, woke Ellie middle of the night. She rolled quietly from the bed to her feet and slippers. Always wore slippers.

Spiders.

Eli was up, too, standing over the toilet waiting for something to happen.

"You're up again, Ellie." He said without looking. "How many nights is that?"

"Too many. I'm tired for no reason at all. Beat. But can't seem to sleep."

"That extra salsa?"

"No. 'Cept my tummy *does* hurt." She wheezed for air.

"Breathing don't sound so good."

"I know." Ellie said standing straight to get more air. "I'll be fine."

Both knew better.

"Maybe we should see your doc tomorrow." Eli said trying to coax himself to pee.

"Easier said than done. He retired you know. Got that new one. Young guy. Kinda hard to just *pop-in*. Need an appointment with this new, young fella."

"I know. But you don't seem right to me. We should see him." Eli said. "Maybe the ER."

"I ain't never *been* right." Ellie laughed.

"Bologna! Always been perfect to me, El." He shook his head, flushed, kissed her cheek. Still not sure if he peed or not. Be back soon enough.

Ellie nodded. Loved the old guy.

She turned to kiss him.

Collapsed sprawling to the bathroom floor.

"Good morning. I'm Doctor Jefferson." He reached out his young, pink and white hand. Perfect teeth sparkled.

Eli took his hand doubting anyone so young could actually *be* a doctor.

Ellie smiled from the examination table. Not so sure she wanted this young buck perusing her private parts.

"My nurse tells me you collapsed earlier this morning. Came to the ER. When was that?" Jefferson asked.

"Couple hours ago." Ellie said.

"We was up peein' . . ."

Ellie shook her head at Eli.

". . . and was talking when she just dropped like a road apple."

Doctor stared at Eli for the longest time.

Then back to Ellie. "Shortness of breath?"

"Yes, some."

"You up often during the night?" Doctor asked.

"Not usually. But, yes. Lately. And as tired as I've been, I can't seem to sleep."

"Hell, I get up four, maybe five times a night to pee." Eli said. "Got me a busted prestate."

"Prostate." Jefferson said.

"Yeah. One of those, too."

Jefferson stared at Eli. Nodded. To Ellie, "Fatigue?"

"I suppose. Not from farm work. Nothing really. Just listless. A different kind of tired."

"Hmm" Jefferson said.

"Hmm, what?" Asked Eli.

To Ellie, "Exercise?"

"Of course. All over the farm. Cows. Horse to groom . . ." Doctor cut her off nodding.

"Smoke?"

"No."

"Good. However, your blood pressure was much too high and notes here don't indicate you're on any medication."

"That's right, I'm not." Ellie said proudly.

"Should be." Eli said.

"Will be." Jefferson added with a smile. "One pill a day. Inexpensive. Any heart attacks or heart disease in your family history?"

"Yes. My father died of a heart attack."

Eli settled back into his chair, his head against the small room's wall as those words were spoken aloud, *died of a heart attack.* Felt a chill. He and Ellie knew the history, but thought by this time, both eighty-eight. If there was to be a problem, it would have occurred by now. Something to warn them beware. A twinge or something. Her father, a bull of a farmer, died sitting on his old tractor plowing a drain curtain ditch along the property line.

"Age?" Jefferson asked.

"He was fifty-eight." Ellie said looking sad at Eli. Knew what he was thinking.

He smiled back at her. Crinkled his chin.

"Ellie," Said Jefferson about to make an announcement, "I don't like the pattern or the symptoms. Family history either. I believe you have the earliest warnings of a possible heart attack. Let me repeat, *earliest warnings.* Don't want to scare you any more than that. It's great that you didn't put off coming in like so many who think they ate too much Mexican food and have indigestion."

Eli laughed out loud.

Ellie smiled at him.

"What?" Asked Jefferson.

"We *did* eat too much at Micki and Roy's last night."

Jefferson smiled. "Done that myself a few times. Nevertheless, good you came in. I'll prescribe the blood pressure medication for you. Here's a list of what I want you to eat going forward. More importantly, what *not* to eat. No more fried foods. Get the fat out."

"What about Micki and Roy's?" Ellie asked.

"Taco salad. Don't eat the bowl." Jefferson said.

"Damn." Ellie said to herself.

"Not to worry, Mother. I'll eat it." Eli said.

Jefferson looked at Eli. "You watch it, too. I'm not your doctor, but best thing you can do is support Ellie eating what she does. Sneak what you want behind her back, but eat *her* diet. Be good for you, too"

"I will. That's a fact."

In the clinic's parking lot, standing at the truck's open door, Eli took hold of Ellie's shoulders. Turned her into him and wrapped her up in his strong arms. He had teared up. "You and me never had any *serious* health issues. Been awful blessed in that department. Never had nothin' that said *trouble ahead*. This getting old stuff ain't all what it's cracked up to be. We're gonna take this serious, El. And if it's our time, remember, I go first. We agreed."

"*We did no such thing, Mister Ragsdale!* Don't you go pulling that shit with me. You go and I might as well be dead."

So much for the sweet farm gal. He thought.

"Same here." Eli said.

"Well?"

"Well. Figure we need to time our heart attacks at the same time." Eli said.

"That's what you figure is it?"

"It is."

She crumpled her lower lip and chin. Hugged him long and hard.

Whispered, "I love you, Ragsdale."

Four

As was their Sunday morning custom, more of a ritual actually, the Ragesdales ordered coffee and sat where they could look out the front of Starbuck's preparing for the other couple to arrive.

Eli sipped his French Roast, Ellie her latte. "Beat 'em today."

"We did." Ellie replied.

" 'Bout time. They been getting earlier and earlier so to be first. Weren't never a race."

"True." Ellie loved listening to Eli ramble on.

"Now they're late. We won't have time to talk."

"There will be time, Eli." She said. "Fact is, here they come."

Big diesel rumbled through the parking lot. Faith Keebler waved frantically like a long lost relative.

Will helped his wife of forever down from the big rig. They made their way through the parked cars across the parking lot into the popular coffee shop. Faith immediately came to the table. Smiling ear to ear.

"What's got you all happified?" Eli asked standing for a hug.

Faith wrapped her arms around him. "You two." She said.

Kissed him on the neck.

Hugged Ellie. To Will standing in line, "Will, get me a scone, too, please."

He nodded. Ordered.

"So. How are the Ragesdales since, what, Thursday?" Faith asked.

The pause was pregnant.

"What? How are you two?" Faith pressed. Concern wrinkling her face.

Will sat. Handed over Faith's latte and scone. Big bite missing. Faith raised her eyebrows at him.

Looking with anticipation at the Ragsdales, "Come on, what?" Faith grew louder.

"Ellie's been to the doc." Eli said.

"What?"

Ellie sipped and leaned back before telling all about their little heart adventure.

"So, what does this mean?" Will asked.

"Not sure until all the tests are done." Eli said. "More tests to go. Some kinda heart probe or something like that. Squirt dye in her heart and look see for narrow spots. Gotta see the heart doc specialist."

"Cardiologist." Ellie injected.

"Yeah. That guy. Next week."

Another prolonged pause. Each sipped coffee. Concern palpable.

"And we pray for His guidance." Ellie said.

"We do." Will said.

Faith nodded.

Eli stared into his coffee cup. A twinge of fear quickly ran its course.

"Enough of that. Hay's baled for the year." Ellie said.

"Yep. Frank will bring by your ration this week. Thursday maybe." Eli said.

"Thanks, Eli. Means a lot to us." Will said.

"Probably mean more to your horses."

"It will for sure."

Coffee done, Eli squeezed Ellie's hand all the way to the truck. Firm enough for her to notice. Hurt some. She said nothing. Understood. Just clung tight.

Neither spoke until the truck's engine stopped in the church parking lot.

Ellie took Eli's wrist, "I'll be okay."

He nodded. Tears filled his eyes. "Scared, El."

"Me, too. Some. But I'll be fine."

"Love you, darlin'." He said.

She smiled, leaned for a kiss.

After a perfect service, Will stood with Eli, both with a handful of cookies. Cup of coffee.

"You okay, partner?" Will asked.

"I think so. Just kinda scares me. The unknown and all. Be okay if it was me."

"Not for Ellie if it was you." Will said.

" 'Spose not."

Five

Buckshot had made the journey to his bale of alfalfa.

Eli and Ellie were nestled under the fir by the river. Heads touching at the forehead watching the river.

Frank Wallace and sons arrived to start bucking the hay. Both Ragsdales struggled to their feet and ambled slowly up from the river into the field. Frank waved and met them as they walked.

"Ya can smell fall comin'." Frank said.

"That's a fact, Frank."

They shook hands. Frank hugged Ellie. She waved at his sons already tossing hay on the flatbed.

"How you two been?" Frank asked.

Eli looked at Ellie, "Fine. Couldn't be better. You?"

"Good. Busier than a horny goat haulin' in hay before first rains. Like it busy though. Good money for the boys."

"Edna?" Ellie asked.

"She's fine. Looking' to the holidays already."

"Dang! Frank. It's only first of October." Scowled Eli.

"Know that. But you walk the halls at Costco and Wal-Mart and they already have Christmas trees, Santas. Lights and decorations and whatnot."

Ellie dropped her head smiling to remember how simple it all was when she was a girl. Mid December trudge through the snow. Cut down a tree. Drag it home and get it decorated. Christmas morning everyone got one present. Lots of food and laughs. "Seems we wanna get things over with before they happen. Everyone's in such a rush."

Both men nodded.

"Coffee, Frank?" Ellie asked.

He glanced at his two big sons tossing eighty pound bales of alfalfa like they were cotton balls. Shrugged. "Sounds good. Usually in the way anywho."

They patted Buckshot as they passed. Old dog didn't budge.

Took Ellie longer than usual to get back to the house. Breathing slow and ragged. Eli held her hand.

"Ya okay, Mother?" Eli whispered.

"I am." Both were concerned.

Frank trudging behind, wasn't so sure either.

Boys got half the field hauled away that day. Left old Buckshot alone on his bale. Would bring in the other half the next day. Frank came back the next day, too. Brought a peach cobbler his wife Edna made.

Brought Edna.

Four sat on the back deck eating cobbler, sipping coffee and chatting until Robert and Walt had bucked all the hay. Saved them each a large slice of cobbler.

Sunset. The long, relaxed day ended with hugs and an empty cobbler dish.

"Dinner at our place soon." Edna said to Ellie who nodded.

"A fine day, El. They all are." Eli said. They cuddled on the couch.

"Thank God."

"Always do."

"Eli. When I go you, you think you'll find someone else?" Ellie said.

There was a pause.

"Yeah, 'spose I will. Don't have much time left you know."

"Really. You'd move on?" Ellie was surprised.

"Sure. Why not?" Eli said.

Ellie pressed. "Got someone in mind?"

"Nah. Figure once you're put to rest, the gals will be lining up down the driveway. Pick me a hot one."

"Sally Walker?"

"Oh, there's a hottie."

"Or Becky Welch from church."

"Too hot for me. Maybe, though."

"Sonja. That lazy redhead at Macy's."

Suddenly Eli's head dropped. Shoulders slumped.

"What?" Ellie asked.

Kidding was over.

"Rather be dead than live without you, El." He sobbed. "I'm hating this."

She clung to him. Held on fast. "Me, too. Me, too. We always knew there would be an end to this ride. It's been a most wonderful life, Eli. Wouldn't change a thing 'cept getting those three angry children of ours to speak to one another. As for you? A woman couldn't ask for a more noble, honest man. We always knew one of us would go. Knew one would go before the other to be with the Lord. Now that time is at hand, more or less. It's hard as can be thinking' one of us will be left behind – alone. It's like a hovering, gray cloud has just joined us and won't blow away 'til it gathers one of us up. I hate it, too, Eli."

Morning found them asleep in each others arms.

Cuddled on the couch.

Six

Snow blanketed the valley.

"Looks like six inches or more, Mother." Eli, bundled head to toe, shouted from the freshly cleared trail to their fir tree by the river. Snow had altered the terrain, much to their delight. Nooks and crannies of the field, river, valley beyond, now smoothed out with a wide butter knife of crystal frosting.

Ellie did not answer. She was taking careful steps on the icy dirt.

Eli shuffled his way down the final slope. Two large, lidded coffee mugs filled with hot cocoa.

"Ya hear me?" He shouted. Didn't need to shout. Quiet as a tomb.

Trumpeter Swans cut the silence with their provocative honk and slapping of wings. Eli watched the V-shape of big swans fly to the nearby lake.

"*Ellie!*"

He approached the tree. Could see one leg askew out from where she sat against the trunk.

Couldn't run. Probably fall. Hurried.

Her head was lolled to one side.

"Ellie. Honey?"

Asleep, she jumped. "What?"

He sighed a quiet *thank You, Jesus* and handed her a mug of cocoa. " 'Bout six inches."

"You or the snow?"

Well, she sure as hell ain't dead.

"Hah! The snow, silly."

"Yes. Looks to be that much." Ellie laughed.

" 'Sides, I ain't been six inches in ten years."

"Is that all it's been?." Ellie laughed out loud. "Best you quit while you're ahead."

"I will."

"Got us an email this morning." Ellie said.

"From?"

"Frank Wallace."

" 'Bout?"

"Oscar Lopez." She said. Sipped her cocoa.

"El! Let's have it."

" 'Member Oscar?"

"Yes."

"Died over the weekend. Wife found him behind the wheel of his car in the driveway. Key in the ignition goin' to the store. Never got the key turned."

"He was the . . ."

"Student body president." Ellie finished.

"Didn't his folks have . . ."

"The Cantina Mexican restaurant."

"You knew it well. Guess I did, too." Eli said with a smile.

"You and me met there often. So young. Crazy."

"We only had thirty-eight in our high school class. How many of us still alive?" Eli asked.

"Lost Beth Allen and Mary Peltz last summer. Connie Small and Robert, ugh . . ."

"Presley."

"Yeah, Presley. Now Oscar. 'Bout fifteen left counting us."

"Damn."

"Seventieth reunion next September. Could have it here at our place." Ellie said.

"Could."

"If we're here."

"We will, El. That's a fact."

"Last night. How many times?" Ellie asked.

Nice subject change. Eli chuckled to himself

"Oh. You think that was me banging around the bathroom?"

"How many?" She asked.

"Six."

"Ain't there some kinda newish medicine you can take for that?" Ellie asked.

"Yeah, all sorts. Complications scare me."

"Such as?"

"My dick will fall off."

"*That's* not good."

"No." Eli said.

"How would you pee at night?" Ellie smirked.

"How would I pee during the day?"

"I don't know. On your head out your nose?"

They laughed til it hurt.

Eli elbowed her. Tossed back his cocoa and struggled to get up.

Helped Ellie up.

Hand in hand they squeezed along the narrow cut in the snow.

Ahead Buckshot lay atop his bale in the path at the crest.

"Look who's waiting for us. Hey, Buckshot. Come on, boy."

Blue Heeler didn't rise. His blue fur beautiful against the white snow.

"Buckshot?"

Ellie petted him. Yanked her hand back.

She looked at Eli, tears exploded from her eyes running down her cheeks.

"Oh, no!"

Ellie nodded.

Buckshot's eyes were closed.

Never opened again.

Hard as it was for him, Eli sat on the thin skin of snow. Ellie the same, cradling Buckshot's black and gray head.

Stroked his muzzle. His oversized ears. Still warm. Swept a hand slowly down his side feeling the chill of his passing.

A snowflake drifted onto Buckshot's muzzle. "I sure ain't likin' this, El. Not one damn bit."

Tears dripped from Ellie's cheek to the dog's fur where they sat repelled by Buckshot's natural oils. She gently rubbed each tear into his fur.

"Hard to bury him in this frozen ground." She sobbed.

Eli choked, couldn't answer. Nodded.

"Could we dig a nice grave inside the barn all protected and such? Or under our tree?" Ellie snuffled.

Eli looked up at the barn. Then back down the groove through the snow at their tree. The fir stood cold, sentinel like, covered with snow. "That's a better idea, Mother. We can come see him every day. You stay with him. I'll get us a pick and shovel. Dirt's not as frozen under the fir's boughs."

"Eli?"

He slowly turned back to her.

Through choked back tears, "How 'bout some mulled wine. Lots of it."

Eli, his shoulders heaving in sorrow, nodded. Bent, patted Buckshot's head. Ellie's, too. Walked crying to the barn.

Ellie clung to Buckshot. Crying a Beatles tune, *Yesterday*.

Took some doing for the old couple to plant their beloved Buckshot deep enough so coyotes couldn't get at him. Roots and all in the way.

Ellie found a speckled, white rock on the beach beneath the fir protected from the snow. Scratched a cross on it. Set it on Buckshot's grave. "Say something." She said to Eli.

He started. Stumbled with grief. Started again. Cried some.

Finally, " 'Scuse us, Father God. Don't usually have any trouble talking to You. Today's a mite different as You must know. It's just that me and Ellie seemed to be surrounded by loss lately. Friends, Oscar and all. Now, our wonderful Buckshot. You know how we loved him. Him us. Know it's one of Your fine plans and we thank You for that. Don't always agree, but take what You give us with blessed appreciation. Like Buckshot here. Was You who brought him to us. We've been eternally grateful. We are. Seems like just yesterday You left that little pup on our driveway by the mailbox. Our life was never the same. Buckshot brought us great joy. We know he'll do the same for You. He loves unconditionally. Likes his ears rubbed. Will eat anything you toss him. Loves banana nipples. You know, the two ends. Ain't much for fetching things. Will sleep right up next to You. Can be a little hot in summer, but real cozy in winter. Ellie and me thank You for his short time with us. Bless him. He's a good one, Father. Amen."

"Amen." Cried Ellie, her voice cracking.

Snow was falling on the way back to the house.

Left Buckshot's bale of alfalfa right where it was.

No one spoke.

Nothing left to say.

Seven

"You just gotta pull the plug, Eli." Will said over his coffee cup. "We've all done it."

"Should." Eli replied halfhearted. "But Brian, here, still plows. You bale."

"Yep." Brian said.

"Brian don't count!" Able said.

"Why not?" Brian asked.

" 'Cause you're an old fool." Said Able.

Laughter.

Will held up a hand. "Now hold on a minute. I'm not hearing commitment here. Eli, you're eighty-eight. Time to hang it up. Shoulda ten years ago. I'll bet your kids think you should."

They might. Thought Eli. Hadn't talked to any of them in over a year.

"You have Frank's sons to do all the heavy work. You rotate like a master gardener. Field yields double most others. Should give you plenty of money to afford the boys to do the work. You and Ellie just sit back under that big fir and relax."

"We could." Eli said.

"But you won't." Laughed Seth.

"Probably not." Echoed Doug.

"Probably not." Eli nodded.

"Shit!" Said Will.

"All seriousness aside, Eli, how's Ellie?" Asked Travis, trying to get caught up after six months in Arizona.

"What have you heard?"

"Heart something or other. Oh, and Buckshot. Sorry about that."

"Yeah. Been tough on us both. Best dog ever. Ellie's heart thing was in October. No problem ever since. Doc says it was a warning shot and to pay attention to just about everything."

"Her doc retired. Preston, wasn't it?" Seth, a retired pharmacist, asked.

"Yeah. Got her a new guy, Jefferson. Seems okay. Kinda young." Eli said.

"Hell, at our age, ain't everybody?"

Laughter.

Eli finished, "He's just a mite pushy for me."

" 'Bout what?"

"The usual we all hear. Salt. Sugar. Meat. Caffeine. Wine. Hell, *livin'* in general. Fool wants to take away all the fun we have left. I mean, we're eighty-eight. What's the point of bein' all powered careful *now*. Maybe shoulda fifty years ago. I figure it's too dang late to get cautious and stop enjoying things we love. Hell's bells, got so little time left, why screw it up."

"Best to listen to him, though." Seth said.

"Yeah. Ya could live to a hundred and ten, don't wanna screw that up."

Eli shrugged with a smile thinking twenty more years just not in his plans.

"Will said you buried Buckshot under your fir by the river. That right?" Brian asked.

"We did." Eli said. Didn't elaborate.

No one pushed it.

Every man at the coffee meet had been in Eli's boots. Knew the pain.

"Well, this bein' our first coffee meet of the new year, what, January eighteenth, I offer a toast to each of us for a great year

---

and good health. We meet here every Tuesday at nine in the morning." Frank said holding his coffee high in the air.

"*Nine!*" Travis howled. Kidding.

"What? Too early for you old timer?" Frank said.

"Some."

They toasted. Couple pushed from the table and said their goodbyes. Frank, Will and Eli remained. Each took one last refill from the waitress. Will turned to Eli. "Not kidding, buddy. Love you like a brother. Park the tractor. Want you around for a long time."

Eli nodded. "Already *been* a long time."

"Yes, it has."

Eli continued. "Frank, what's a fair price for your boys to work the field? All of it, all the time."

"Boys won't take money from you, Eli. Value you and Ellie too much to dent your livelihood. I'll talk to them about some trading. Alfalfa for whatever. 'Member, Robert's got the biggest organic garden in the county along with his upstart organic dairy. Walt's all about dairy and chickens. Both doing well. You been loaning them your equipment for years. It's time for payback. I'll talk to 'em both. We'll work something out for you two."

Eli nodded his appreciation.

"And you ever decide to sell your place, I believe Walt's always interested." Frank said.

Eli winced. Held his gut.

"What is it, Eli?" Will asked.

"Just never thought about livin' anywhere else. Leave the farm. But Frank's right. Day will come. Damn!"

Will looked over at Frank. Both shrugged some. Will a hand on Eli's shoulder.

"Long way off my friend. Loooong way off."

Eli smiled weakly, nodded.

But he knew, *long way off*, wasn't.

Eight

What Coffee Tuesday was to Eli, Knitting Thursday was to Ellie.

Thursday's, like so many other days for the Ragsdales, was full of ceremony and tradition.

Day started at five-thirty. Took Eli all of twenty minutes to shave and shower. Toss on jeans, t-shirt and sweater. Then boil water and set two cups up for brewing coffee. Side-by-side, sitting on a tri-folded towel, two mugs with a Melitta filter sitting it a Melitta black plastic filter holder.

Then, in old slip-on sandals, he'd trudge to the edge of the gravel driveway, crunch down for the local daily paper and make for the house.

Then patiently wait for Ellie. Paper open, cups on the kitchen counter.

Summer, the sun would rise to his delight.

Winter, it remained dark long after his Ellie arrived.

Which she did around sevenish.

She would appear in the small, narrow kitchen, slide into her seat all sleepy while Eli re-boiled the water to pour over the fresh grounds. They loved their coffee. His black.

Hers loaded with enough milk and sweetener so to mask the coffee taste.

"Where are ya on the sweater this week?" Eli asked.

"Same as last."

"Which was where?" Eli said hoping Ellie wouldn't say she already told him last week.

"Told you last week."

"*Ellie!*"

She smiled her *love* smile. "I'm joining the sleeves to the main part. Been putting it off. Hard part for me, the locking stitch and all."

"You've done it before. All them sweaters for the grand kids."

"Yes. I have. Just seems a little more difficult than before."

"You getting tired of knitting?"

"No. It's not that. Just all the effort it takes to get up, get goin'. Having to have you drive me. Just all of it. Hate putting you out so."

Putting me out? Sheesh! Eli thought.

"Ellie, we been over that. You know I love doing anything for you. 'Specially this knitting thing 'cause you enjoy it so much. Least whys you did."

She nodded. Sipped some coffee. Glanced across the red vinyl floor at Buckshot's dry water dish still where it always sat. She sighed.

Eli noticed, but said nothing. He'd already made his sigh over the dry bowl.

After their coffee and a shared a muffin or bagel, they'd get in the truck and drive the six miles to old downtown and Bessie's Knit Shoppe. Eli would walk Ellie in, flirt with the other seventy and eighty-something ladies, then walk four blocks to the Farmer's Co-op for more coffee. Usually alone. Wave at whoever honked at him. Never looked up, just waved.

"Morning, Ellie. Eli." Bessie said. Her cherubic, red cheeks overly made-up. Eyeliner askew. Blazing red hair stacked up atop her head. Frizzed out all around.

"How's Bessie today?" Eli asked.

"She's fine." Bessie said, not really engaged in the conversation, unloading a box of yarn to inventory.

Ellie, more subdued than usual, shuffled to the back of the store where the *girls* were already stitching and purling and blocking over coffee. Staccato chatter. She sat, hands curled in her lap over her knitting bag. She nodded around the table. They all nodded back continuing their chitchat.

"You joining the sleeves today, Ellie?" Cheryl asked not looking at her knitting. Hands moving a mile a minute.

Ellie nodded.

"How's Eli? Still missing his dog?" Sylvia asked.

"Yes. He . . . *we*, miss Buckshot everyday." Ellie said.

"When our Shelty, *Mitsy*, went off to the dog farm in the sky, me and Able were just crushed. I remember how that felt." Marilyn said.

Ellie nodded.

"They become such a member of the family."

"Like children, really."

Ellie nodded.

"Always hate losing a member of the family."

Several nodded.

Losing a member of the family. Ellie thought. She sat, hands still clasped in her lap. Eyes tearing up.

"Everyone hear about Bud Coltrane?" Asked Betty knowing full well no one knew.

"What is it *this* time?" Cheryl asked. " 'Nother bar fight."

"No. Not the usual. I'm told he's on the wagon."

"What? When? Since the taverns closed 2 a.m. this morning!" Marilyn giggled.

They all chuckled. Knitted.

"Old fart's too old to be hanging out in taverns anymore." Cheryl added.

"Or fighting."

"Word is he's sober as Pastor Bob. It's been almost two weeks." Betty said.

"Wow! Two whole weeks."

"Two in a row?"

"Should have a party for Bud."

"BYOB."

Laughter.

"But he's *not* drinking." Betty said.

"Then he's *not* invited." Laughed Cheryl.

Betty sulked.

"Could rain tomorrow."

"Need it."

"Anyone hear from Anne Betz?"

"Vacation. Went to someplace hot in the south."

"Phoenix."

"For sure? Phoenix?"

" 'Swhat I hear."

"Too hot. Now, take Chicago."

"*You* take Chicago. Filthy place."

The chitchat buzz was steady like a power lawnmower. As if she had adjustable hearing aids, Ellie gradually tuned them out. Sat feeling detached from the group. Isolated. Really *was* tired. Missed her Buckshot something terrible. What did the doctor call it? She couldn't remember. Her arms felt heavy. Lead-like. Ached some. Without a word, she stood, took her bag, turned, walked out to the sidewalk.

Chatter rambled on behind her.

She walked the four, very long blocks to the Co-op for Eli. Inside she was greeted by a cheerful employee. She didn't acknowledge. Wandered the coffee tables.

No Eli.

She felt panic well up. Hurried up and down each aisle.

"Ellie?" Came a voice from the sky.

She stopped. Looked around.

"Ellie! Up here."

She tipped her head back. Smiled at Eli on the second floor mezzanine.

Her man smiled back.

"You looking for me?"

She nodded. Will leaned out over the rail next to Eli. Waved.

She nodded again. Waved.

"Me and Will be right down." Eli said.

She waited by the stairs ruffling a rack of scarfs.

"Knitting over?"

"It is for me. Just couldn't get into it. All that gossip. Chitchat. Rather be with you."

Eli smiled at Will, then at Ellie. Arm around her shoulders, "Me, too, honey." He turned to Will, "Good to see you, Will. Catchu later."

"Later. Bye Ellie."

"Will. Hi to Faith." She waved.

The four block walk back to the truck was slow. Neither spoke.

In one hand, Eli held Ellie's knitting bag. Her hand in the other.

"You look a little pale, El. Sure you're okay?"

"I am. Let's get home. Like a nap." Ellie said.

"I'll be thinking on dinner while you rest. Thinking chicken of some kind."

"Be nice. Thanks."

Nine

Pastor Bob was closing in on fifty.

Looked twenty-five. Lean and athletic. Bubbling enthusiasm. Wife the same.

Eli and Ellie always came to the nine o'clock service. Seemed fresher than the eleven o'clock.

Eli parked in the same slot every Sunday. They sat in *their* seats every Sunday.

If they missed, the seats remained empty.

Eli turned the key, the truck's engine coughed quiet. "Coulda dropped you off right at the front door, El."

"Coulda."

"Why not?" Eli asked knowing her response meant she was glad he didn't drop her off.

"Like the short walk holdin' your hand. Like folks to see that. Seems folks don't do enough of that these days. Holdin' hands. I love your hands, Eli. Rough and weathered on the inside. Reminds me of all the years you've given me everything you have. Back of your hands as soft as a baby's ass."

Eli nodded. Smiled. Squeezed.

Held her hand with gusto. Walked a little taller to the front double doors.

"Morning, Marilyn."

"Morning, Ragsdales. How you two?"

"Fit." Eli said with a hug.

Inside they slowed to say hello to most everyone they passed to their seats. Eli helped Ellie sit, but continued to schmooze his way around the congregation. Stopping below a tall picture of Jesus to say hello to the Son of God. Done, he dropped heavily onto his seat next to Ellie.

"Fit?"

"Huh?"

"You said *fit* to Marilyn at the front door. What's *fit* about us?"

Eli paused, looked around and took a breath. Turned to Ellie. Took her hand.

"Ellie, dear, I love you such a way it's too danged hard for me to explain. Knots my stomach. Have since third grade when you bounced that tether ball off my head."

Reminded, she smiled in thought.

"Every Sunday we settle in here. Smile and joke with folks we know. Not really friends, just folks we know who share a love of Christ. Sing a couple songs. Cry some. Say a silent prayer. My prayer is always thanks to God for pairin' me up with the likes of you. *Fit?* Oh, yeah. Sure, we got legs, knees, damn hips, other stuff that's beginning to fail, but my heart and soul more *fit* than ever. At peace with God. Peace with you, too. Only been one girl in my life. Been blessed to live all these years, most of it with you. Fact you love me back in so many ways just makes it all that more wonderful."

She smiled. Tear trickled around her nose. Kissed his cheek. "Fit. Okay, Eli. We're fit."

Eli sat back feeling spent after so much talk. Felt good, too.

Held her hand in his.

Ten fifteen the service ended. Coffee and cookies.

Eli was a cookie fool if there ever was one. Homemade. Store bought. Cookie dough. Crumbs. No matter. Man loved his cookies. Today there was an abundance of pecan wafers.

Made a fool of himself

"Eli, I swear, you must be made up of half cookie fixin's." Pastor Bob said. "While Ellie's visiting the ladies room, like to have a word with you."

Eli nodded.

"I got word from Marilyn who heard from Betty, one of Ellie's knitting group ladies, that Ellie wasn't herself Thursday. She wandered out from her knitting without even a goodbye. I know she's been under the weather. She doing alright?"

"Been tired a lot lately. Not sleeping well. Doc warned her of heart issues and to watch her diet. May just be she's more worried about it than she's letting on. As you know, Buckshot, our dog, died. That didn't help. Broke her heart. But since you and others noticed, might mean I don't see it. Being so close and all. I'll pay closer attention with that in mind. Thanks, Bob."

"I'll add her near the top of my prayer list." Pastor Bob winked.

Eli nodded. He'd thought all Ellie's little changes were just *him*. Now others were aware of it. Cause for concern? Maybe.

Best watch her. What she's eating. Little more walking. He thought as she approached from the ladies' room.

Took his hand. Odd smile.

Making a joke, "Everything come out okay?" Eli asked.

"Funny! Yes. Thank you." Like she would answer a stranger.

Closer. Gotta watch her closer. Damn!

Ten

"Her doc says she needs a cardiac cath . . . cathet . . ."

"Catheterization." Said Seth adding way too much sugar to his coffee.

"Yeah, that." Eli said.

"Run a hose up your ass." Travis mumbled.

"*No!* Not up your butt. Sheesh, Trav, this is serious stuff." Seth said. "It's a catheter, and they insert it in an artery in the groin or arm. Pump in some dye and shoot an x-ray or some such. Tells 'em what they need to know."

Eli stared blank into his coffee.

Seth put an arm around his shoulders. "Not to worry, Eli. They find anything during the procedure they fix it. Ellie's strong. She'll be fine. My mother had that. They found nothing."

"So why do it?" Travis asked.

"To be safe and know for sure." Seth said.

"Just kinda scary is all." Eli said.

"We'll all be here for you. Ellie, too." Will said gripping Eli's forearm.

Their eyes met across the table. Eyes glistened.

They were like brothers. Close.

Like twins sharing feelings. Sensing. Understanding.

Eli choked back a sob. Sipped his coffee.

With crinkled lips, Will nodded he understood like no one else.

Eli knew he did.

"No reason to suspect anything yet. She's whipped through all the other tests so far." Seth said breaking the silence. "As a pharmacist I can tell you there is a litany of drugs for her as well. She'll be fine."

They were all so sure. Eli thought.

So why didn't it feel right to Eli. Everything was upside down. Old Buckshot was gone. Favorite foods couldn't eat anymore. Social Security check's shrinking. His hips and shoulders shot, crunched when he moved. Politicians all seemed like they only cared about themselves. Couldn't farm anymore. Loved farming. Turning the soil. Smell of cold earth. No more horseback riding. Damn terrorists. Ease back on the red wine.

What the hell!

And Ellie. She balanced on a precipice with this heart thing. Eli's stomach lurched at fleeting thoughts of being alone. Getting old was just not what he'd thought.

All we ever talked about is getting old. Thought Eli to himself realizing they *were* old.

"And how 'bout that Obama?" Brian asked with a laugh.

"Brian! No one cares. His honeymoon will be over in a blink."

"Probably."

"It's okay, guys." Eli said lifting his head. "Most of you been through the same, one way or another. Cancer here, new hip there. Travis, two knees. It's just new to me. Me and Ellie. Just never thought . . ."

"We'd become obsolete?"

"Shit, Frank!"

"Well, just sayin' . . ."

"We ain't last year's tractor."

"Feels like it sometimes." Frank said.

"Yes. It does." Eli said with a smile, realizing this conversation path was his doing. "But we are all blessed men and still young in some ways. Just falling apart is all."

"That 'sposed to make us feel better?"

"Some."

"On a lighter, more productive note, *Eli*." Frank said, steering the conversation.

Eli turned to him.

"Robert and Walt be over tomorrow to lay out the fields for planting. You said you had to rotate. If it's okay with you and Ellie, me and Edna like to come along. Maybe join you two, and sweet, old Buckshot, of course, under the tree. She's baking zucchini bread."

"She bringing it warm?" Eli asked.

"Straight from the oven."

"Hey!" Barked Will. "What are we, chopped silage?"

"How 'bout Edna bake three loaves, and you *all* come over to the Ragesdales 'bout ten tomorrow morning?" Said Frank.

They all laughed, some volunteered to bring another treat.

Will stood, "And tomorrow me and Frank will bring along something special for you and Ellie."

"For?" Eli asked.

"Just never you mind. A surprise. And don't you dare take it the wrong way, you old fart." Will said.

"That's *Mister* Old Fart to you, my friend."

The laughter was healing all the way into the parking lot.

They departed in different directions.

Eli sat in his truck mumbling to himself.

All we ever talk about is getting old.

Eleven

Wednesday came soon enough. Ragsdales both woke early. Eli set the coffee out. Ellie waited for the wood stove heat to reach the kitchen.

They sat together sipping and humming. "You look rested, Mother. Good night?"

She nodded through the coffee's rising steam.

Both held their respective cup in two hands to warm their cold fingers. Watched out the kitchen window across the lawn and driveway at the brightening eastern sky. Hint of blue, pink.

A smile smoothed crossed Ellie's velvety face. Soft lips. Still wrinkle free. Natural, rose colored cheeks. Little fuzz Eli loved.

"We got us two hours before friends arrive." Eli said.

"And don't forget the *surprise*." Ellie said. She winked.

"Too old for surprises." Eli groused.

"You behave. These are your lifetime friends doing something special for you. For *us!*" Ellie scolded.

"I hear ya, Mother. I'll be good. Bagel?"

She nodded. "Zucchini bread comin'. How about we share just one."

Eli took one from the bread box. Sliced it in half. Butter. Toaster oven. Jam. They loved their bagels *just so*.

Frank, Edna,their two sons and daughter, Cindy, arrived first. Put his truck the far side of the parking area. Wasn't long before Will and Faith swung their big flatbed onto the gravel drive.

An overstuffed, red, velveteen loveseat and small coffee table jiggled along on the flatbed.

"What's that Will Keebler up to?" Mumbled Eli bending to look out the kitchen window more clearly.

Ellie stared blank at the tiny table tottering on the flatbed. "Not a clue."

Eli pushed open the screen door and marched straight to the flatbed. Frank and boys were helping Will unload the loveseat and table.

Then they hefted a flat, hay skidder from the truck. Heavy duty, braided cable was hooked to each leading edge secured to a large eye screw.

Frank called to Eli, "Get your fancy old 9N out here. Back up to this cable."

"Frank? I mean, what . . .?

Frank waved him off, "Just humor us, Eli. Get the tractor."

Ellie joined them.

Edna, then Faith, hugged her.

Eli's tractor growled from the barn and soon emerged from the sliding door. Belched smoke getting into position. Frank hung the heavy cable over the PTO assembly. Will and sons put the loveseat and table on the skidder.

Will walked up to Ellie. Held out his arm. "Ma'am. Will you do me the honor?"

She took his arm all the while eying confused Eli seated on the Ford.

Ellie sat on the loveseat.

"Eli. If you would. Please hop down here and take the seat next to your lovely bride of three-hundred years." Will laughed.

Shaking his head, Eli stepped on the skidder and cuddled up next to Ellie. Touched foreheads with a smile. Draped an arm around her shoulders.

"Driver. If you would please."

Robert Wallace, Frank's oldest son, ran, jumped to the tractor seat and slid it into a very low gear. The tractor hummed, coughed. Moved ahead out into the field towards the fir tree.

Eli squeezed Ellie's shoulder. She looked at him, eyes asking.

"I don't know." Eli said to the unasked question.

A weathered bale of alfalfa sat alone at the edge of the crest to the water.

Both Ragesdales nodded a heart thought.

Took a slow ten minutes to the tree. Robert swung out a bit and stopped the skidder beneath the tree's boughs. The others, who had walked alongside the procession, escorted both Eli and Ellie to their well-worn seats on the ground beneath the fir tree.

"I bet Buckshot's wonderin' what the hell's goin' on." Eli whispered to Ellie.

Ellie smiled at the thought. Continued watching the others set up for the zucchini bread and coffee, which was now being driven down the long gradual slope by all the others who had arrived.

Sixteen in all gathered under the fir by the river. Walter Wallace switched on a portable radio to a local Christian music station and soon zucchini bread, butter, and coffee were distributed to all.

"Ya like it?" Will asked.

"What?" Eli said.

"The skidder. Loveseat and coffee table."

"Love it."

"It's yours. Now, Eli, before you get all uppity wacko on me about insinuating you and Ellie are getting too old to negotiate this field, I want to explain. We made this so you and Ellie can get down here just a tad bit easier. Know it's a long walk and walkin's good for you, but we didn't want anything to take this tradition away from you two. Ya just hook up the skidder, Ellie sits and you drive. You can sit beneath the tree or stay on the loveseat. Whatever, but it's for you two from all of us."

"With lots of love." Edna chimed in.

Eli looked at Ellie who had that look to tell him, *"Relax and go with it. No harm done."*

Eli struggled to his feet, stepped up to the skidder, turned back to look at Ellie sitting, smiling, beneath their fir. He smiled and held up his coffee cup, "To the best friends anyone could ever ask for. It's perfect. Thank you so much."

A cry of laughter and celebration followed.

Edna slid down the fir tree next to Ellie, "You like it?"

"I love it. Good idea. 'Tween you and me, Eli's been struggling to get down here lately." Ellie whispered.

To Will and Frank, Eli murmured, "Good idea. 'Tween us men, Ellie's been struggling some to get down here lately."

"We love you guys, Eli. Just wanna help."

"Yep. That's a fact."

Twelve

Thursday Ellie slept well beyond her knitting group's meeting.

Eli made his coffee and slipped to the barn to have a look at the skidder once again.

As much as he quietly resented the part insinuating they were too damn old to hoof it through the rough plowed field from the house to the river, the thought was very nice.

Of course, they were.

Too old.

Thirteen

Ellie settled into the soft, velveteen loveseat. It was old. Little spongy, but she was comfortable.

Eli started the Ford, pulled from the barn into the drive and turned down the field for the fir tree.

"Comfy, Mother?" Eli yelled over the tractor. Glanced back.

Ellie smiled. Nodded. Waved for him to go on.

Three weeks they'd had the skidder. Ellie loved it. Today was no different.

She worried some about winter. The rains and snow. Wind.

Eli knew her concern.

"Not to worry, Mother. Have a plan." Eli said.

"An *Eli* plan?"

"Yep."

"This one gonna work?" She asked.

"Mother! Don't they all?" He laughed.

"No."

"*Wicked* woman."

"Yep. What's the plan?"

"Roof."

"On the skidder?" Settled in the soft powdery dirt beneath their fir, Ellie turned against the bark to glare at Eli.

"Sure. Why not? Nothing fancy. Just protect the loveseat and table. You and me."

Ellie thought on it. Hummed her approval.

"And when it's really raining, maybe even snowing, we could still come down. Just stay on the skidder under the roof." He said.

"Be cold."

"That's a fact, Mother."

Eli built the roof. Three sides like lean-to. Slowed the old tractor some, but was much warmer. Wind protected.

Ellie loved it more than she expected.

Will and Frank, after a needling inspection, put their stamp of approval on it.

Tested it first snow in late November. Skidder slid fine across the light skin of snow. Ellie, all bundled up in blankets laughed the entire trip to the tree.

"Like a sleigh ride." Ellie said.

"That's a fact."

"Not as cold as I thought." She said.

Eli cuddled up with her out of the falling flakes. Big, sloshy ones. Poured their coffee from a thermos. Put an arm around his bride of seventy-two years. Kissed her chilly cheek, pink from the cold. "Don't get much better'n this, Mother."

'Cept be lot better if Buckshot huddled here, too.

Through the rising steam from their mugs, under the fir boughs, across the river, two deer, a doe and her fawn, dug for remnants of summer's grass.

"No, Eli. Surely doesn't get much better."

"Don't call me Shirley."

"Eli!" She laughed.

Deer looked across at them. Doe cocked her head. They moved on.

Weren't many days that winter the Ragsdales didn't take the ride. Ellie was saddened their children never came by, even during the holidays. Christmas would have been particularly fun driving grandchildren back and forth to the river.

New Year's Eve Ellie fell asleep under Eli's arm sitting on the loveseat by the fir tree. Resounding echoes from nearby fireworks woke her a little after midnight.

"Hello, Mother."

"What happened?"

"You fell asleep."

"How long?"

"Not long."

"What time is it?"

"Happy New Year." Eli said.

"Hope so." Ellie replied.

Fourteen

Eli's eighty-ninth birthday in February started at Tuesday coffee with his buddies. Ended at Will and Faith's for dinner. Twelve friends sat around, mostly talking, as usual, about aches, pains, government, doctors, AARP and getting old. Diapers. Assisted living. Grandchildren. Weather. Some gossip and the untimely passing of Pastor Bob's father, a longtime friend of Eli's.

"Known Bob, Sr. for . . ." Eli thought, slipped off into probing the distant past, high school, grammar school. "Pre-school?" He said.

"Pre-school? Howled Will. "No *pre-school* during the Civil War."

Everyone howled.

Eli doubled up laughing. "You should know. You old pelican."

Will, laughing, pointed a finger at him.

Pleasant night with old friends ended just before ten. Ellie seemed more tired than usual.

Eli used that as an excuse to leave.

She fell asleep in the truck on the way home.

Next morning they slept in. Both achy and tired.

Ellie slept until shortly after eleven. Found Eli sipping his second cup of brew. "Been up long?"

"No. Not so much. Coffee?"

She nodded. Eli poured boiling water over the grounds.

"Nice party." Ellie said, rubbing sleep from her eyes.

"That's a fact."

"Fact is the whole day was very nice for you on your birthday." Ellie said.

"It was. Nice friends. Good birthday." He nodded in thought watching the water filter down through the grounds. Gave Ellie her coffee.

"Like to sit under the tree today. Visit some with Buckshot." She said.

"Sure. How 'bout lunch by the river." Eli said.

She nodded with a low hum. Smiled after her first sip of coffee.

"You okay, Mother?"

She didn't answer.

"Mother?"

"Yes?"

"You okay?"

"Really tired."

"See the doctor?"

"Don't think so. Just need to go easy some. It was late last night."

Ellie napped at noon. Rose at one-thirty. Dressed and found Eli in his small office checking emails.

Hugged him from behind. Glare from the screen was bright for her eyes. Kissed his head. "Want me to fix our river snack?" She asked.

"Think we oughta pass on that. Thirty degrees out."

"Eli, I'm rested. Feel better. I'll make us some treats to share and coffee. We can bundle up."

"Chips?"

"Sure."

Two-thirty Eli pressed the start button on the Ford 9N and it coughed. Sputtered. Quit.

Tried again. Same.

"Maybe we eat here in the barn." Eli said. Hoping.

"You'll get it. Always do."

He tried. It kicked over.

He pulled up by the fir tree. Both said hello to Buckshot. Eli spread a tarp at the base of the tree and then several warm blankets. Helped Ellie from the covered loveseat to the base of the tree. Seemed much too cold to sit on the ground, but Ellie insisted. She sat with slow grace. Pulled two of the blankets over her.

Eli fetched the lunch. They ate.

"You bring sugar, Eli?" Ellie asked, clutching her coffee mug.

"*Damn!* Forgot." He stood. "Be right back."

"Don't bother Eli. It's fine." Ellie said, but knew he'd go.

He did.

Just took eleven minutes.

Arriving back he swung the tractor around. Killed the engine.

"Got your sugar, Mother." He said from the tractor seat.

Was very quiet. Breeze had quit. Snow, too.

River current slowed.

"Ellie?"

The silence was chilly.

Heavy on his shoulders.

Eli slid from the tractor seat. Ellie's right leg visible from where he stood. The back of her head was against the tree, leaning to the right on her shoulder.

"Ellie! No!" He expected her to say something. Anything.

To lurch awake.

She didn't.

Eli eased around the tree. Stepped over Buckshot. Came around to Ellie's left.

Her hands clung tightly to her empty coffee mug resting on her lap. A drifting fir needle had fallen on her gloved hand by her thumb.

Eli knelt before her. Thumbed back her hair from across her left cheek and eye.

Both eyes were closed.

Peaceful. Warm smile.

Eli removed a glove. Her skin already cooler than normal.

She was beautiful as always.

"Damn!"

He swung around to his bottom. Cuddled up tight next to her. Put an arm across her shoulders as always. His forehead against hers as always. Took the mug from her hands.

Put sugar in it. Milk. Poured her coffee. Set it on the ground next to her.

"Got your sugar, Mother." He whispered.

Poured his own coffee.

Sipped it. "Good coffee, Mother. Real good."

Eli Ragsdale sat with Ellie and Buckshot long into the night. Too stunned to cry. Hardened some by time, the passing of so many others he loved. His arm fell asleep across her shoulders.

Drank all the coffee.

Prayed some.

Finally cried. Often.

Thought good thoughts.

Owl swooshed into the fir above. Hooted.

River babbled.

Dairy cows mooed back and forth across the icy, snow covered valley.

Life continued around him.

Eli sat with his bride. Unsure what to do. Cried more. Sobs off and on through the hours. Had many long chats with Jesus making sure Ellie was comfortable. Grilling his Lord why *she* had to be first.

"Weren't the plan, God. As often as we speak, You think this is what I wanted? No, Sir! 'Course I ain't no old fool. Figure You spared her the grief of my passing. I get that. Appreciate it. I suppose it's okay. Know *You* make the plans, but I figured I was real clear on this. S-she was my one and only love. My sweetie.

"M-my . . . rock."

Owl hooted.

Dog barked.

"My beloved rock." Eli whispered.

Fifteen

Eli woke with a shudder. Unfulfilled sleep. Glow of the clock said four-fifteen.

Dark. Snow cold outside.

He slid out from under the sheets so not to disturb the bed. Slippers, robe tied tight. Shuffled to the living room to start a fire.

Made the cold trek down the frozen drive to retrieve the paper.

Got water boiling, poured his coffee. Sat at the table looking at his reflection in the window.

"Been a cold winter so far, Mother." He said quietly.

He sat back. Steam from the mug warmed his forehead.

He turned to the stove.

Ellie's coffee mug sat. Melitta holder, filter. Waiting for her.

As always.

He shook his head. Shivered. And like every morning since her passing, Eli cried. Put away the empty filter and holder. The mug. *Her* mug.

An aimless time of day filled with silence. Too cold and dark to go outside. No to-do list. No meal to ponder. No one to help or coddle. No other noise but his own.

No laughter.

He didn't eat.

Knew he had to snap out of it. Moping and all.

Walked to the living room. The bookshelf.

Ellie's ashes in an urn.

Kissed the silver urn. "Morning, El. Miss you."

Brushed away a tear.

Will would be there in a few hours. Pick him up for the Tuesday coffee meet. All his coffee buddies were so careful what they said. Will, his best friend since forever, tiptoed on thin ice with every word. Will also knew Eli and Ellie's erstwhile adult children, all retired and living in opposite directions around the state, called or dropped by rarely. Short, sullen visits. They missed their mother. Hardly knew their father. Knew he preferred being alone. Like everyone else, they too, afraid to say anything wrong. Something insensitive.

Pastor Bob arrived at six-thirty. He was more real. He brought prayer. Doughnuts. Some straight talk.

"You need anything, Eli?" Pastor Bob asked.

Eli looked at him smirking the obvious.

"Yes. I want her back, too. For you." Bob said. "But you know what I mean. A man can cry and mope himself to death if not careful."

"Dying *now* wouldn't be a bad thing." Eli said.

"No. It wouldn't be bad when it's time. Not your time yet."

"How do you know that?"

"Prayer."

Eli shrugged. "I get it. I'll be fine. Time's all I need. *And* my Ellie. Need her most, I guess. Thanks, Pastor. So much water under mine and Ellie's bridge. Just hard to consider each day without her. But I'm working on it."

"You *will* heal, Eli. You *will* move on, but that's not to say you won't miss Ellie. Feel her warmth and presence every minute of every day. In fact, you *should* feel her presence. Her . . .touch."

Eli nodded. "I do. I surely do."

Don't call me Shirley. Eli could hear Ellie say.

Will arrived. Spoke with the departing pastor. They shared concerned looks. A handshake.

"You save me a doughnut?" Will asked Eli in a strong, upbeat voice. Trying once again to get Eli out of his mourning funk.

"Yep. He brought a dozen." Eli said.

Sitting, Will pulled papers from a tattered, leather briefcase. "This is from Frank's boys. Schedule for your field and a proposal for the crops. Looks good to me."

"You want a hot dog?"

"Hot dog?" Will asked adjusting to the u-turn of topics. Surprised at Eli's spirit. Glad.

"Yeah. Bought me some Mariner dogs at the grocery store. Big. Loaded with salt and cholesterol. Got me some hoagie buns. I'm gonna have two."

Will glanced at his watch. Seven. Coffee meet with the boys at nine. He'd already had coffee, cereal. "Sure. Why not. But only one."

"Wimp!" Eli said getting up.

Will laughed. "Old buddy. Starting to sound like the man Ellie loved so much."

Glad you think so.

"That's a fact, Will. Pastor Bob got me thinking and Lord only knows, *boy does He,* Ellie'd be mad as hell at me when I get up there if I just pine away sobbing for her til I keel over dead. No, sir. She's up there fixin' up Heaven, lecturing Jesus on some things that need settling and taking care of Buckshot. Least ways, that's how I see it. Ought to honor her some by being myself best I can."

Sure hope Will buys this. May get him off my case so I can feel sorry for myself.

"What got your head on straight?"

"Pastor, some. Made me think I'm not totally done down here. Loved that gorgeous woman with all my heart. Every breath. Miss her every waking moment. Can't wait to hold her again. Was born to be with her. Care for her. Figure there's some unfinished business for me before I go else I'd *be* gone already. Best I straighten up some."

"Glad to hear it, my friend."

Thanks for buyin' my bullshit.

"Will. Thanks for bein' there for me. I love you for that. You are a brother for sure."

Will nodded. Choked up some.

Later each and every member of the coffee meet was delighted to have Eli back.

Or so it appeared.

The morning talk was good, supportive. Productive. Two of the others had lost wives over the years. Had much to share they'd been holding back until now. Eli leaned on their every word. Knew they only wanted to help. Best he could do was listen. Some of it was good.

Though his stomach churned with every mention of Ellie.

Will dropped him off after a stop at the grocery store.

More hot dogs.

Eli set the bag down on the kitchen counter.

Exhausted, he moved to the kitchen table and sat in Ellie's seat.

Looked around at the emptiness. Listened to the silence.

Been a long day putting up a false front. Just figured it was best for all those who wanted to help.

Then, head in hands, Eli leaned forward, folded onto his lap.

Screamed Ellie's name amidst an outburst of tears.

Sixteen

Frank, Walter, and Robert Wallace arrived early. Pulled up behind the house next to the barn. Eli came to the back door, waved and they all approached.

"Morning." Eli said.

"Eli." Walt and Robert echoed.

"Come to get this field started, Eli." Frank said. "Place we can go over this?"

"Come on inside. Coffee's brewing as we speak."

Frank couldn't help but notice how tired, pale, Eli looked. Clothes wrinkled. Weeds already making a presence around the driveway and porch.

Eli, slumped a little lower than usual, led the three younger men through the mud room to the small kitchen.

They sat. Coffee was good. French Roast. Dark.

Eli's scones not as good as Ellie's. Not bad with enough jam.

"Gonna prep the field before we plow. Some new humps here and there. Gotta move that big boulder near the crest before the drop to the river." Walt said.

Eli sat listening.

"I'll service all the equipment today if that's alright with you, Mister Ragsdale?" Robert said.

"Ah . . . sure. Sure. Fine." Eli said.

"Then we'll plant." Walt added.

"What boulder?"

" 'Scuse me, Mister Ragsdale?" Walt asked.

"Boulder. What boulder?"

"Looks like a big black rock before the slope." Frank said. "Big, egg-shaped one. We saw it comin' down the driveway. Never been there before. Kinda weird, but no problem moving it. 'Swhy we're here to get the field ready."

"Ain't no boulder there. No rock, neither." Eli insisted.

The three Wallace men shrugged and looked at one another.

Eli stood and bent to the window to look. Bad angle. Scuttled out the back door.

Shaded his eyes to look down the field. Morning sun had cleared the distant mountains. Still couldn't see a rock. Field smooth as Ellie's cheek.

"There." Pointed Robert.

On his tiptoes, Eli still shook his head.

"Drive me." He said.

They piled into Frank's truck and started down the field. Hadn't gone very far.

"Stop!" Eli said. Got out.

Moving as if approaching a wounded tiger, they followed Eli down the middle of the weather beaten field.

Smooth as Ellie's cheek.

Except for a big, black rock at the crest before sloping to the river.

Big.

"*Damn!*" Eli said, walking slowly around the shiny rock. His image a soft, blurry reflection in the deep, obsidian surface.

"How in the *hell* did this . . . *could this* get here?" He yelled.

Wallace men all shook their collective heads in silence.

"Weren't dragged." Eli said kicking at the ground around the boulder. Looking up, "Rocks just don't drop from the sky."

"Not ones this big." Frank said touching the rock's smooth texture.

"That a river rock? Walt asked.

"Kinda." Frank said.

"Don't expect there's been any rivers through here lately. At least not last night." Eli said. He was serious.

On his knees, Frank probed some at the base of the rock. Went deep.

"Well, hell's bells, somebody dumped it here." Eli said.

That's crap. Ain't no deep tire tread marks.

"Gotta move it before we start the field." Robert said.

"That's a fact." Eli said. "I can get it off here this afternoon with the Ford. You boys go ahead and make your plans. The rock will be in the river by the end of the day. Any other grooming to be done, you can do tomorrow."

Back in the kitchen looking over a rough drawing Robert made for planting the field, there was prolonged silence while they finished their coffee until Frank spoke.

"I remember my father running in from the field when I was a boy. Yelling about a missing tree. We had us a row of tall, old cottonwoods for a windbreak on the south fence. One morning Pa took off to work and was back in no time. We all looked out. There it was. A gaping hole where one tree used to be. Looked like a six-year old kid missing a front tooth."

"Where'd it go?" Walt asked.

"Don't know to this day. Tree was gone, roots and all like a carrot pulled out by a giant."

"Ya heard nothin'?" Eli asked.

"Nope. That's the mystery. Never heard a sound."

Eli rubbed his chin.

" 'Member similar odd story about a river up and changing course during the night."

"Happens all the time, Eli."

"Not like this. River was more a creek middle of summer. Ran east to west on the *north* side of old Ben Crossman's farmhouse. Had him a small bridge to cross it. Woke one morning and the river was running east to west on the *south* side. Had to build a whole new bridge and everything."

"But . . . how, I mean . . ."

"Yep. Strange one." Eli said. "So, a big rock appearing ain't totally unbelievable. Strange as hell, but shit happens. Stuff that can't be explained. Yeah, that rock's inconvenient, damn near impossible to figure, but there it sits."

They chuckled some. Finished their coffee. Eli walked to the barn for his Ford.

"Have the rock moved in a jiff." He mumbled to himself.

Eli was confounded for sure. More importantly, he was thrilled. Had something to do. A job that needed being done. Simple task. Drop the Ford's bucket into the side of that stone and push it over the crest. Ought to roll the rest of the way into the river.

Ought to.

Ford reluctantly turned over. Eli bounced across the smooth field to the rock while the others worked in the barn with Eli's other equipment.

"You are one damn big rock, mister." Eli said to the elephant-sized boulder. "But I gotta tell you, ain't nothin' my Ford can't move. Best you get comfy for a bath."

Eli lowered the front bucket meeting the rock at ground level. Planned to dig straight under and tip the rock enough to roll it down to the water.

"*Clunk.*"

Rock was deeper into the ground than he'd thought.

Eli pulled back and lowered the bucket back some from the rock. Hit something solid far below the surface. Using the bucket, he pulled back three feet of prime top soil from around the rock. Slid down from the tractor seat.

Frank arrived as Eli squatted shaking his head.

"Looks like this rock's been pushed up somehow." Eli said. "Goes deep."

Frank examined it. "Yeah. It does."

"Damn strange you ask me." Eli said.

"Damn strange."

"One big rock.

"That's a fact."

Seventeen

The following Sunday, Eli crumpled into a pair of pants and a shirt he thought suitable for church, slid behind the wheel of his truck and backed out from the carport. In the rear view mirror a silky fog nestled around the looming black boulder at the crest.

That thing move?

Eli stared in the little mirror for the longest time. Shook his head. Turned the truck around. Drove around the planted field. Slid from the seat and walked to the rock.

Still sat where it had been all week.

More or less.

Earlier in the week Eli had dug an exploratory trench completely around hoping to find the bottom.

Trench was filled in.

Rock had turned ever so slightly from its northerly direction, now facing more northeast. Facing more towards the fir tree.

If it had a face.

He touched the surface. *Smooth as Ellie's cheek.*

His reflection was more clear. Sharper. He could see himself in the ebony surface. Took off his glasses and moved in close. Leered deep into the blackness.

Only saw his eyeball.

Shook his head on the way back to his truck.

Dynamite will move that thing!

Church was routinely exciting. Uplifting. Full of promise, information – a message to share. Eli more focused on the rock than God. Missed it all.

"You seem to be somewhere else this morning, Eli." Pastor Bob said.

"Some. I guess."

"I'm always here if you need to talk."

"I know. Thank you."

"Eli."

"Yeah?" Eli's sad eyes rose to meet those of the Pastor.

"It takes time. Give it time. God will help if you ask."

"I do. I have. I will." Eli nodded and left. Met Will and Faith at his truck.

Faith hugged him. Will the same.

"Why don't you join us for dinner tonight, Eli." Faith said.

"Can't tonight. Busy. Thanks."

Eli crawled up to the seat of his big diesel. Engine roared and he was off.

"Man can't be *that* busy." Will said. "Too old to be too busy for dinner. Mind's somewhere else."

"He's lost, Will." Faith said. "Loved that woman fierce."

"He did."

"Another time. I'm sure he'll be fine."

"I'm telling you, this rock goes to China." Eli said to his coffee mates.

"How big?" Asked Brian.

"Big as an elephant." Eli said.

"Ya can't move it?" Able asked.

"No. Hell's bells, even Frank couldn't move it with his big old New Holland."

"Seems to go on down forever like it's attached to the Great Wall." Frank said. "Damnedest thing I ever did see."

Will turned to Frank, "Budge it at all?"

"Bucket low as possible, nothin'. Pushed it. Nothin'. Me and Eli locked a series of chains to it. Pulled it. All we did was tear up the field. Rock don't even quiver."

"Dynamite?" Asked Seth.

Eli looked at each familiar face looking back at him. "We could. Been thinking on that."

"Tear the hell outta yer field." Brian said through his glazed doughnut.

"Done some stumps with it." Able said.

"Me, too." Frank said. "Scary stuff, you ask me."

"Anybody have some?" Eli said, halfway hoping no one did.

"I do." Will whispered.

"Well?"

"Be more fun than talking politics for another hour." Travis tossed in.

"It would." Will laughed.

"That's a fact."

Hour later eight men, some stumbling slow in the sod, others too old, drove, made their way to Eli's rock.

"Damn! Sucker really is big." Seth cried out bending his head back looking at the top of the rock.

"It is." Eli sighed.

"You sure about this?" Will asked.

Eli hemmed. Dragged his tired body around the rock. His image crystal clear staring back at him. Over the last few days, the rock had gradually turned. Eli put a hand on the end now pointing its egg-shape directly at the fir tree. *Smooth as . . .*

"Got three sticks. We use 'em all?" Will asked.

. . . Ellie's cheek.

"Eli? Use 'em all?"

Eli put his other hand on the rock. Closed his eyes.

The men gathered behind him some. Shrugging. Whispering.

"Eli?"

Eli slumped to his knees. Hands held in prayer. Head down.

Not a whisper. Tears dropped off the gray stubble on his chin. From behind, all seven men watched Eli's reflection in the black rock.

Acknowledging Eli may need to be alone, his friends slowly peeled off one at a time. Only Will remained, sitting in the soil far behind Eli.

In time, he, too, quietly walked to his truck to leave.

Only a cool evening chill woke Eli. He leaned to one side from his knees to look around – alone. Stiff in every joint. Too dark to see the tree, the river, the house, barn. Stars popped in and out of the clouds. Breeze was cold. River quiet.

Eli pressed against the rock to get up. Felt warmth emanating from the surface.

"Eli."

Familiar voice. He whirled around squinting into the darkness. Almost fell.

Whirled again. Stumbled his way around the rock. "Who's there?"

No answer.

"This ain't funny!"

He turned to the rock. Its shape barely visible in the murky black field. "That you, Ellie?"

Shit! Goin' outta my mind.

Touched the rock again.

Warm.

Pulled his hand back. Stepped away. Looked up to the heavens. Around the surrounding darkness.

"Father God. Sir. You *messin'* with me? I know I haven't been myself since Ellie's passing. Been trying. Really. How would *You* feel if someone *You* loved . . .Oh, my God! Forgive, me Father. It's just that, that . . . I miss her so much."

He broke down. Tears flowed like the nearby river.

A scraping noise startled him. A chill shook Eli to his core.

"Who's there?"

"Eli." A whisper so soft Eli thought it was the breeze.

He jumped away from the rock.

"Eli."

Voice was clear as a cloudless autumn day. Crystal.

"Ellie?"

More scraping noise directly in front of him.

The rock crunched in the soil. Heaved. Bumped Eli.

He cried out.

Passed out in a heap.

Early next morning, worried how they left him, Will and Frank found Eli huddled asleep against the rock.

"Coffee?"

Eli rubbed his eyes. Pressed against the rock. Still warm.

"Yes. Thanks."

"You been here all night, haven't you?"

" 'Spose I have." Eli sipped. Looked long and hard up at the hovering rock.

Frank walked the perimeter of the luminous boulder. "This thing moved."

"It did." Eli said.

"But?"

Eli shrugged. Will and Frank looked at one another. "But?"

"Rock's gonna stay right where she is." Eli said. Smiling.

Not so pale now.

"She?" Frank said.

"She."

Eighteen

"Eli!" Bessie cried out. Arms wide to embrace. "It's so good to see you. I'm so sorry about Ellie. We miss her so much down here. She was such a joy."

Eli, trying to smile, slowly made his way around the stacks of yarn, knitting needles and How-to Books. He handed Ellie's knitting basket to Bessie. Behind her, the usual cacophony of voices had stopped.

Five gray haired women stared at him like he was naked.

Marilyn Stover, Able's wife, quickly rushed out to hug him. "Eli. Eli, Eli. We have so missed Ellie. How are you doing?" She overwhelmed.

Damn! This is awkward.

"Fine. Brought this in." Eli handed the basket to Marilyn.

She looked it over.

"Was hoping one of you ladies could finish this sweater Ellie started. Only needs the arms added to the body part. I think it was for me."

Marilyn wiped a tear, turned to the group still peeking out the backroom door. They nodded in unison.

"Of course. We would be honored."

He nodded. Stood like a child waiting for a treat.

"Oh, um, couple weeks?" Marilyn said.

Eli nodded. "That would be fine. Thanks, Marilyn. Thank you all." He turned and left.

Marilyn returned to the group. "I didn't know this was for Eli."

"Me either. Looks to be way too small." Char said.

"Maybe it wasn't for him."

"Wasn't." Bessie said returning to the back room. "Was for her."

"What should we do? We finish it as it is? Sure won't fit Eli."

"Could make another."

"Yes! Bigger."

"How 'bout we finish this one *and* make another? One for him"

"Why?"

"I don't know. Something special for Eli?" Sylvia groped.

"No. Don't think so. He'd have his. What would he do with the other?"

"Ugh! Not good. Matching sweater for your deceased wife. Not so good."

"No. Not so much."

"What then?"

"Make a new one. Extra large so be sure to fit. One of us just hang onto this one."

"And the mysterious rock we've been hearing about?" Marilyn asked.

"What *about* the rock?"

"I'm not knitting a sweater for some damn rock."

Everyone stared at Marilyn as if a second head had emerged on her shoulders.

Glaring back, "Able says Will and Frank think *Eli* thinks the rock *is* Ellie."

"No shit!"

"*Sylvia!*"

"Well, I'm just saying . . ."

"Heard some about this." Char said. "It's true."

"Ellie is a rock?"

"No. Eli thinks she is."

"That's not good."

"He must be losing it."

"Ellie's a rock?"

Long, thoughtful pause.

"So. Who wants to start this sweater for Eli?" Bessie asked.

After dropping off the sweater parts, Eli drove north. Traffic stacked up behind his truck, crawling along in the slow lane up the interstate.

Horns honked. Cars swerved.

Tempers flared.

He waved with a smile.

Others weren't so polite waving back.

Eli took the exit leading to the small lake and valley north across the river behind his property. Parked in a graveled turnout by a locked barbed wire gate. Stabbed and sliced himself several times working his tired body between the fence lines. The walk would be difficult. Field had recently been plowed. Huge chunks of soil flopped up, leaving deep ruts to trip and fall.

He did.

Often.

And each time he fell, he dropped the silver urn with Ellie's ashes.

Persisted until an arduous hour later, sweaty, hands bleeding, Eli stood the opposite side of the river across from his and Ellie's fir tree. He promptly slumped to a round river rock. Tired. Legs cramped.

Across the water and behind the fir, up the incline at the crest, the rock.

The reflective boulder sat like a hen warming her eggs. Nestled into the dirt. New grass starting to appear around her base.

Rock had moved again. Was now facing directly at the fir tree. *That's a fact.*

Eli shook his head in amazement. Seemed impossible that huge boulder moving. He loved it.

And it scared him some, too.

He grunted to his feet. Eased down the steep embankment to the water's edge. Slow current. No salmon. He opened the urn and held it up to the sky. Held it to the black rock across the river. The fir. He took them all in. All those special things he and Ellie so dearly loved. Buckshot. House and barn roofs barely visible far up the hill.

"Only place that seemed right for you, Mother. Came to this side of the river so I could see where we sat and all those things we ever loved and shared. Figure the slow current will take some of you to our side of the river. Some to the lake. Maybe some to the ocean.

"Kept some of you for my nightstand. Hope that's okay."

Squatting, he slowly, tearfully, let Ellie drift from the urn. Some of her lifted into the air and swept away. Eli looked across at the rock.

"If that's you, Ellie, I hope this is what you meant by putting your ashes in the river. Does seem right. But I gotta tell you, folks think I'm crazy. You bein' a rock and all."

Tired from the walk, the emotional disposition of Ellie's ashes, Eli sat on the river's edge watching the gray remains spread and drift. Closed the urn.

Big salmon bubbled by.

"Took your sweater into the girls to finish. Thanks for starting it. Gonna be nice come winter."

Rock sat silent.

Looked to be staring through the tree straight at him.

He stared back.

"You see me, don't you? Shoot. 'Course you do. How's God these days? I figure you have Him straightened out by now. Jesus, too. Not like They need any help or nothin', but you were always so good with people you probably have something good for Them, too. Oatmeal cookies. You should try those. Bet those two will love 'em. Oh, the Holy Spirit. Dang! Three of 'em for you to, you know, do stuff for. I'm rambling, Mother. Like always. Maybe I *am* crazy. Miss you. Love you."

Rock sat silent.

Eli creaked up to his feet. Fought his way up the river's bank. Looked across the wretched field at his truck what looked to be a hundred miles away. Groaned.

What was I thinking?

By the time he reached his truck a light rain had moved into the valley. Clouds roiled in the wind. He ached in places he didn't know he had.

"And walnuts, El. Put walnuts in those oatmeal cookies."

Nineteen

Rain pounded so loud on the truck's roof, they had to shout across the front seat Will had parked in Eli's gravel driveway close to the road. They stared down the long, rutted drive, between the barn and shed out to the field.

"He's been out there every morning this week." Will said leaning to his wife.

"How long?" Faith asked.

"Don't know. Don't stick around. Hate to bother him. He'll think we're bein' nosy."

"Will, you're his best friend. He won't mind."

"He might. Neither of us ever been where he is before."

They stared.

The rain and a lazy fog kissing the ground made it difficult to clearly see the tractor far down the field in front of the rock. Couldn't see Eli huddled inside the three-sided lean-to he built around the loveseat and table.

But he was there.

Eli heard the truck. Heard it every morning all week. Hard for a big diesel engine to be quiet.

Will's diesel engine.

Thought about stepping out from behind the shelter of his lean-to. Wave.

Didn't.

Not sure why.

"It's Will again, Mother. He's not sure what to do with me. Hell's bells, I'm not sure what to do with me. If I was to video this and watch it on the television, I'd be calling out the Looney Bin Cops. Don't know many folks hereabouts who sit in the weather, shivering from the cold, talking to a rock."

Abruptly Eli felt warm air wash over him like he'd just opened a hot oven to check the evening's meal. Covered him head to toe.

Inexplicable.

"Thanks. I needed that."

Behind him Will's diesel caught. Eli could make out the crunching gravel and accelerating RPM's until they faded over the hill west of his property.

"Frank's boys be here tomorrow. Start working the field. They'll work around you. Won't bother you none."

Eli shifted his position, sitting more in the corner where the loveseat arm curved to meet the back.

"Gonna sit some, Mother.

"Love you."

Twenty

Bessie saw Eli drive by. Pull to the curb to park.

She ran to the back room. "Ladies, he's here."

Betty and Cheryl poured coffee, dished the coffee cake.

Eli opened the front door. Warm inside. He hurried to close out the cold.

"Good morning, Bessie. How are you this fine spring day?" He was beaming.

Bessie smiled with raised eyebrows. "Why Eli, you sound chipper today. I'm fine, thank you. You?"

"Ohhh, Bessie. Couldn't be better. Well, *could* be, but I'm fine. That's a fact."

Bessie motioned for Eli to pass through the store to the backroom. An empty chair, Ellie's usual chair, was turned out for him to sit.

He did.

Everyone nodded, smiled, said good morning.

Cheryl placed a cup of coffee and a hot piece of coffee cake slathered in butter.

"Thank you, Cheryl. Looks mighty good."

Eli's cheery disposition disarmed the women momentarily until Marilyn stood and passed a big white box to Eli.

Red bow wobbled on top.

"The sweater?" He asked.

They nodded in unison.

"Yes. And we want to see it on you, too." Marilyn said.

He took it out. Examined it front and back. Carefully inched his glare at the knitted crew neck. The tight connection of the sleeves to the main body.

The finish at the waist.

He looked up with a grimace. Met each face stoically. Suddenly smiled.

"It's beautiful. My Ellie sure could knit. Thank you so much for finishing it for her. Means a lot."

Guilt swept the group, each reaching for her coffee or cutting a mouthful of coffee cake. Most eyes were wet.

"Put it on." Bessie whispered.

He did. Tugged it down at the waist. Brushed it smooth across his tummy. "Fits perfect. Better'n I thought it would. Looked a little small when I brought it in. I was wrong. Fits fine."

"Looks handsome on you, Eli." Sylvia said.

"Yeah. Sure does." Marilyn added.

"Ellie will like it." Eli said.

Ellie will like it.

There was a pronounced pause of eerie silence as each woman digested what Eli had just said. They had all heard about Eli sitting in the weather in his lean-to with the rock. Thought the black orb was Ellie. Word was he talked to her.

Bessie broke the silence, "I'm sure she will, Eli. She'll love it."

Twenty One

From the day Ellie departed, the three Ragsdale children kept an appropriate distance to allow their independent and oft times private father, time to collect himself. It was easier than sitting with him with nothing to say or share. No one knew better than they, how their father loved and protected his Ellie, their mother. How he treasured his time with her to the point of ignoring others around him – even his three children. He had been a good father. Dedicated, devoted, but preoccupied. But protected his time with Ellie Elizabeth Thornton. They were inseparable always. As children, it took time to understand the devotion at their expense. As adults, in time, Will and Sarah grudgingly accepted it. Benjamin not so much.

When the three, Will (named for Eli's best friend, Will Keebler), 68, Sarah, 66 and Benjamin, 62, met to determine a game plan for Eli and the family farm, it was precarious thin ice for them to discuss, even in his absence. And they had difficulty exploring anything serious with one another.

Stangers.

"He'll *never* leave. He'll die there. I can see him flat, face-planted on the kitchen floor. Coffee mug shattered in his hand. Dead." Scoffed Benjamin twirling a spoon in his coffee.

"*Benjamin!*" Howled Sarah. "He's our father. How can you say that?"

"Yeah, easy Ben. He may be old, but he's not dead." Will said.

"Come on. We all know how he thinks. Works. Even with Mom gone he won't know we're alive. He'll want to be alone for friggin' ever. Did he call any of us to be help with the ashes. Shit, didn't call me. Had to hear it from Sarah. Hell, he may never call us. And one day we'll get a call from Frank or Will he's been found under that damn fir tree. Dead. I can see it comin'." Benjamin droned on.

Will nodded agreement. It *was* possible.

"We *have* to approach him on this." Sarah said, scowling at Benjamin.

"Good luck with that!" Benjamin said. "Rather approach a raging bull head on than Pop with *this*."

"Thing is, he's still capable at eighty-eight. Hasn't run over anybody with his truck, . . ."

"*Yet!*"

" . . . can still plow a field, cook, dress himself, bathe. All that stuff they do for you in an assisted living facility." Will said.

"And he knows he's capable. Slowed some, but still managing out there all by himself. You can't tell him otherwise. How could we take that away from him?" Sarah said.

"We could start by taking away his keys and truck." Benjamin said.

"Might as well shoot him." Sarah said.

"*That* would solve everything." Benjamin laughed.

"This isn't getting us anywhere." Will said. "We just have to sit him down and get his thoughts. Work *with* him. Not against him. I for one would like to get closer to Dad before he dies."

Before he dies. Sarah teared up nodding. Of the three of them, she had been the closest to her father. Close enough, she thought, to understand Eli and his profound love for her mother.

"One thing I'd like to clear up." Benjamin said, standing. Pacing.

"What?"

"This mysterious rock we keep hearing about. And believe me, folks from here to there are talking about it. Like it's a temple of worship or something. Bart Webster passes Pop's farm every day on his way to work. Says Pop's tractor and that lean-to thing are out in the field parked up next to a huge, black boulder. Morning and night. Either of you two seen this rock?"

"No. Heard about it just appearing out of nowhere, but hadn't heard *that*." Will said. "Guess we should get out there and see it for ourselves. I mean, we've all been out there to see him since Mom's memorial."

Long, uncomfortable pause.

"Haven't we?"

"No." Benjamin mumbled.

Sarah scowled at him.

"How many times you been out there?" Benjamin asked.

"Once." Sarah said. Head bowed. "Will?"

"Couple times."

"You saw him? Talked to him?"

"Drove by."

"My God. What *great* kids we are."

"What about the rock?" Benjamin asked again.

"Wasn't there that I know of last time I drove by." Will said.

Sarah hemmed a moment, "I talked to Faith Keebler. Told me she and Will parked in the drive. They thought they could hear Dad's voice out in the lean-to."

"Talking to who?"

"Himself. We all talk to ourselves. Dad's no different."

"He's talking to the weird rock."

"*Holy shit!* Pop's flipped." Benjamin yelled.

"*No. He. Hasn't.*" Sarah said. "He's lost the one and only love of his life. She was his heart and soul. They were so in love, it's hard for *mortals* like us to comprehend. She was his life. His comfort zone. We all should be so . . . *flipped*."

"You know what I mean."

"I do, but get real. We have to respect Dad and what he must be feeling. Alone. Deserted. Tired. Possibly wishing he had gone, too."

"So? What are we gonna do?"

"I'll call him tomorrow. Tell him I'll bring dinner and you two to visit."

"Whoa. The three of us . . . together?"

"Yes."

"And if he says no?"

"We go anyway."

Twenty Two

Little spring chill in the air when Sarah drove them to the farm the next morning. She'd talked to her father and he was looking forward to their visit.

"Okay. He wasn't thrilled we were coming . . ."

"Big shock there." Benjamin groused. It was too early for him.

" . . . but understood some issues need to be addressed. We didn't discuss details."

Her truck made the final curve off the hill west of the farm. Before them, flat farmland, the Ragsdale farm ending at the river.

Ahead, Eli's tractor and lean-to just pulling out from the barn.

"What now? There he goes." Will said.

"Let's head back to town. Come another time." Benjamin said.

"No!" Sarah said. "We do this today. This morning."

She slowed for the turn into the Ragsdale drive. Pulled up and crept behind Eli on the tractor. She stopped by the house as they watched him circle the black boulder seated at the crest before the river. He pulled the lean-to abreast the rock, killed the tractor engine. Tugged his baseball cap tighter and slid off to the ground.

Disappeared behind the lean-to.

"Oh, *that* rock." Will said.

"Shit!"

"Now what?"

"Hate to walk out there. Seems to be his private time."

"His whole life was his *private time*."

"Private with Mom."

There was a long, thoughtful pause.

"Maybe you just said it. *Private with Mom.* " Sarah said.

"Huh?"

"Well, yes. He was a private man. Buried himself in his work. Farming, tending his garden, butchering beeves. Seeing to it we and our wonderful mother always had what we needed. *Always.* Remember, it was his way to provide for us. It's what worked for him. His comfort zone. There's no guidebook to raising children. He stayed focused. Had his nose-to-the-grindstone all the time to feel like he had done all he could to provide."

Men sat quiet in thought.

"Anybody here ever go hungry? Not have a warm coat in winter? Or a bed of their own to sleep in? Anybody?"

The two men looked at one another. Looked down.

Benjamin paled some.

Sarah continued. "And were either of you denied an opportunity to play soccer? T-ball? Ever told we couldn't afford something? Denied a good pizza dinner? He coached you two how many years? Play volleyball at the Y? Go to dances? Swim at the Y? Who was there for driving lessons? Cooking classes in our kitchen?"

"Only made cookies and oatmeal. Okay, scrambled eggs."

"Hot dogs."

"But he *was* there."

Men nodded, shrugging as if they'd forgotten *those* times.

The car windows were steaming up. "Let's go see him." Benjamin said.

A warm wind swept the valley. Southwest wind off the distant ocean. Rain would follow.

Sarah huddled between her taller brothers. Will put an arm over her shoulders. They reluctantly made the walk around the growing field to the crest and followed it to the lean-to.

They stood working up the nerve when quietly from inside the lean-to, "Good coffee this morning, El."

Sarah held up a hand asking for quiet.

"Not comfortable listening in." Will whispered.

Sarah nodded she agreed. Shrugged. Peeked around the corner of the lean-to.

Eli was looking straight at her.

"Hi, Sarah. We've been expecting you."

Twenty Three

We?

Will and Benjamin curled around Sarah facing Eli. Both leered around at the black boulder looming high above them. Benjamin stepped forward. Touched it.

"Real smooth. Huh, Ben?" Eli chuckled.

Benjamin didn't respond, but rather turned to face the rock. Put both palms on the surface and ran both hands slow, up and down. "Warm."

"Yep." Eli smiled.

Sarah sat next to her father. "Dad we've been thinking . . ."

" 'Bout me and the farm?"

"Yes." He caught her off guard.

"And what have you three cooked up?"

"Nothin', Dad. Mostly we want what's best for you." Will said.

"And your mother." Eli said.

"Dad . . ."

Eli cut her off. "Boys. Sit."

Light rain began falling. Will sat on the skidder deck at one end of the loveseat. Benjamin the other. They all faced their father much like a kindergarten class faces their teacher reading a book.

"Figure you three have heard all the stories how I'm *flippin' out* talking to a rock."

Sarah and Will glared at Benjamin. He shrugged.

"Yes. We have."

"And I 'spect there are some oddball ideas from some folks that I think this here boulder is your mother. That true?"

"Yes. Some."

"Pop. Where'd it come from?" Benjamin asked.

"Mystery to me. One day it was just . . . here. Runs deep. Can't be moved. Turns by herself."

That got everyone's attention.

Turns by herself.

Her*self.*

"Herself?" Will said.

Eli let out a long sigh. "Look into that boulder. What do you see?"

"Myself." Will said.

Sarah nodded.

"Yeah. I see me, too. Real clear."

"Ben, you touched her. How'd she feel?"

She?

"Warm."

"What came to mind?"

"*Shit!* Mom!"

Will and Sarah's jaws dropped. They looked at Benjamin. At Eli. The rock.

Both got up and reluctantly placed both palms on the boulder.

"Shit!" Will said.

"Oh. My. God." Sarah cried. Her voice trembling.

"But . . . ?"

Eli stood and walked to the rock. He, too, placed both hands on the boulder.

Benjamin joined them.

"Before any of you kids says *shit* again, what do you *feel*?"

Sarah fell to her knees. She hunched up in heaving sobs.

Will followed. He, too, choking back tears.

Benjamin closed his eyes. Pressed his chest and arms against the rock. Hummed like his mother always did when she loved something too much to speak.

"You three still think I'm losin' it?"

Crying too hard to speak, Sarah stood. Turned. Folded into her father's arms.

He held her like never before.

Boys made it a group hug.

"I've missed you guys." Eli said.

"Now. Want you three to sit on the loveseat."

They did.

Eli turned to the rock. Bowed his head in prayer.

His three adult children had no inkling how to pray. Just never had time for any of the church stuff their mother and father loved so much.

"Kids. Listen."

They each turned an ear to the boulder.

It sparkled a light from just across in front of Eli's face.

"Sarah." It was a faint sound. Whisper with an echo. Could have been mistaken for the wind sweeping up from behind the lean-to.

Sarah's eyes popped open. Searching.

"Will."

"Benjamin."

Eli stood, "Stay on the loveseat."

He slowly walked around behind the seat and his children.

"Eli."

Eli's image in the rock began to separate from the three on the loveseat. A soft, yellow aura traced the perimeter of his reflected image on the rock.

Another image materialized next to him.

She was half behind Eli. A hand on his shoulder.

Warm smile was all Ellie's.

Sarah folded forward into her lap. Face in hands.

Will fought to not cry. He did.

Benjamin was more intrigued. "How is this remotely possible, Dad?"

Ellie answered. "Your father and I have a bond beyond anyone's imagination except the Father's."

"No limitations for Him." Eli said.

Benjamin turned to his father behind the loveseat. Ellie was not there. He quickly turned back to the rock. There she stood.

"Amazing, huh Benjamin?"

All he had left was a nod.

"But, why? I mean, I've never heard of this in the news. Read anything about mysterious rocks emerging from deep within the earth representing past loved ones. Why now? Why you two?"

"Ben. Ben. Ben. Always the inquisitive one." Ellie said. "None of you three will ever experience the depth of love and devotion your father and I have been blessed to enjoy. An experience like nothing ever before for anyone ever before."

"Sounds like a stretch, Mom. In all of history? How do you know that for sure?" Will asked.

Ellie hummed. "Oh, from where I've been, I know. For sure, I know."

"But I love my wife. Deeply." Will continued.

"Yes. Yes you do. And I'm proud of you for your steady and faithful heart, Will. You've made some difficult choices along the way, and they were all the right ones. You are a shining star, my son."

"But I'll never have what you and Dad had?"

"No."

"Me neither?" Sarah asked solemnly.

"No, sweetie. Not that you won't enjoy loving another with a true and faithful love."

"Well, shoot. Guess that means I'm outta the picture, too. Two failed marriages and all." Ben quipped.

"Don't be too hasty, Benjamin Ragsdale." Ellie said. "Your heart has time."

Sarah and Will turned to Benjamin. Back to Ellie in the rock.

She was gone.

"Dad?"

"She's gone for today. Ain't it great to have her here to chat with?"

Stunned, the three simply stared a blank face at the rock.

No comment.

"Aw, come on you three. It was terrific. Do it everyday. Visit with your mother. Coffee. Occasional doughnut. Bagel. Your mother loves bagels, you know."

Sarah wanted to ask. Didn't.

Eli stepped from behind the loveseat to face his children. Each looking a bit pale and lost. "You came to find out why I was *flippin' out*. You came to help me decide which dang retirement home to move to and when to sell the farm. You came to turn me out to pasture."

"Yep. We did." Benjamin said. "Shoot, Pop, I came to argue and moan."

"Change your mind?"

"Totally."

Sarah still hadn't collated what had happened. Will sat stunned.

Finally Will stood. Stepped to the rock. "Friggin' impossible. But I saw it."

"Heard it, too." Sarah said.

"I know folks in town talk about it." Eli said. "Best you keep today to yourself. Media would love this. Science would love it, too."

"Geraldo would go nuts for this."

"Oprah."

Eli stiffened. "This isn't for *anyone* but us. Am I clear on this?"

Sarah and Will immediately nodded.

"Benjamin!"

"Yeah, Pop. Just for us."

Twenty Four

No one had spoken until Sarah rounded the last turn into town.

"Coffee. Need some coffee." Will said.

"Starbuck's." Benjamin said.

They continued on until Sarah eased the gear shift into Park in front of the coffee shop. They sat side by side staring out the front windshield into the shop. Folks sat reading the paper. Sipping a latte. Many on laptops. A long line stood through the center.

"I know what Pop would say."

"What?"

"It's crazy to stand in line for ten minutes to pay four dollars for a cup of coffee."

"He would."

"Stand in line?"

"Say that."

"That's a fact." Sarah said.

They laughed at that and got out of the truck.

Together, they stood in line for ten minutes to pay four dollars for a cup of coffee. Huddled tight at a rickety table surrounded by strangers who would never believe what the three adult children had witnessed earlier.

Finally, Will spoke. "So. What do you make of that?"

"Sure took the wind out of my sails." Benjamin said.

Others nodded.

"Can't move him out. Shit. Can't ever let the farm out of the family. I mean, Mom's out in the field."

"Yes. By God, she is."

"He must have." Will said.

"What?"

"Done it?"

"What?"

"Put Mom . . . the rock, you know, in the field."

"You mean God?"

Will nodded.

Got no argument.

"A miracle."

"Yep."

Long, thoughtful pause.

"We'll have to give this some very careful thought. Dad has to stay in the house. Farm remains in the Ragsdale name. But when dad goes, what then?" Sarah started to cry. Will touched her arm.

"We rent it." Benjamin tossed out.

"Could."

"And the field?"

"Wallace brothers have more than once said they'd maintain the field as long as we needed them. Works for them. Mortgage is paid. House could just sit empty."

"Field mice. Rats. All move in."

"Not good."

"Then rent the house. Wallaces work the field and keep the harvest. What's leftover, we use to pay the taxes."

"I could move in." Benjamin said.

"Leave your little place on the slough?"

"Yep. Hate to leave it, but do it for Pop."

"And Mom."

"Definitely."

"Can we build?"

"Tear down the house?"

"No. Can the property be divided equally so we could, you know, build new houses."

Sarah and Will tumbled that around in their heads. Each had a family, small children, a house to sell. A spouse to consider.

Finally Sarah spoke, "We could plat it. Three, forty acre parcels all on the river. Sure. It's possible."

"What are we saying here?" Asked Will.

Sarah looked into her coffee cup. Twirled it. "Let's be hypothetical here. Each of us sells our respective homes. One of us moves in with dad." She looked at Benjamin who was divorced and no children. "The other two build new homes on their respective plots. Wallace boys farm the land. Dad can stay in the house as long as he wants or, Heaven forbid, he passes away."

"Means one of us gets a free house." Benjamin said.

"Okay. To be fair, we build two and divide the cost three ways. Maybe toss in some remodeling of the old place. Whatever we do, divide it three ways."

"And the rock. Mom?"

"What about her. That's sacred."

"Fence her in?"

"Sure."

"Okay. Enough brainstorming for today. Let's think on this and get back."

"Soon."

"Yes. Soon. Like to take our best idea to dad for him to think about."

"It *was* amazing."

"Yes. It surely was."

Don't call me Shirley.

After the kids drove off, Eli returned to Ellie in the field.

She had reappeared.

"Guess that confused the hell outta them, huh, El?"

"Yes. But most importantly, it certainly brought them together nicely."

"That the plan?"

"Yes."

Eli got more comfortable on the loveseat. "What's the rest of the plan, Ellie?"

"Honey. I'm so glad you asked."

Was long after dark before Eli fired up the Ford for the barn.

Smiling as he was, the chill of night didn't seem to bother him.

Twenty Five

Folks talked, passersby gawked. Joggers slowed.

But well into summer Eli Ragsdale never missed a single day huddled on his dilapidated loveseat curled against the *Big Ass Boulder* as so eloquently noted by one suspicious neighbor across the river.

Weather warmed. Field grew.

Frank Wallace and sons kept a good distance from the rock.

Crows flew over. Landed. Marched stiff-legged in the mowed grass around the black rock.

Never landed on its tempting, shiny surface.

Behind the scenes, Eli's three children pursued their plans for the Ragsdale farm. Sarah working with city planners, city zoning and county engineers. Time and money eventually divided the 120 acres into three equal parcels of land, each fronting the river. The original home site and gravel drive to all three remained as it was in the middle.

In the process, the three Ragsdales agreed to name the properties E&E Estates.

Eli was informed of each step and glowed with approval.

"Love the name, guys." Eli said from the loveseat. "Ellie loves it, too."

"You think we'll ever see her again, Pop?" Benjamin asked.

"Yes."

"When? Been nearly six months since the first time."

"Soon. I can assure you. Soon."

Sarah settled in next to Eli on the loveseat. "Gotta bring you up to speed, Dad."

Will poured himself more coffee from the thermos. Held it up to Eli asking if he wanted more. Eli shook his head.

"We've been working the plan some and everything has fallen into place as we've been discussing. Everything but some red tape with city planners and permits. Kinda holding things up a bit."

"That's good and bad. Do you need me to talk to the city for you?" Eli nodded.

"No. We need to do this ourselves, Dad." Sarah said.

"Time for me to move in with you, Pop." Benjamin said carefully. This was a part of the plan the three had deliberately omitted from project updates. None of them sure how their father would accept the invasion of his privacy.

"Know that. Your room's vacuumed and dusted. Fresh coat of paint. Same color you picked in high school. Did the same to the bath. New toilet, too. You can come anytime you like. Me and your mother just been waiting for you to get the courage to ask."

Sarah, Will and Benjamin studied their dad's joyous expression as he spoke. He was having fun at their expense. All were a little taken aback by his anticipation, lack of resistance. Not to mention his unflagging support and preparation.

"Painted?"

"Vacuumed?"

"New toilet? Will laughed. "Who did all that work for you?"

Eli first grimaced, frowned from ear to ear. "Will! I'm only *old*, not dead. I did it. Been nice to work on a project for my kids again. Ellie loves what I did and you can move in today. If you want."

"Okay." Benjamin said eying both Sarah and Will with a disbelieving shrug.

"Crews here Tuesday next week to clear driveways to both new parcels. Thursday they begin site preparation for the two new houses."

Eli nodded like it was no surprise. "The driveway spurs will break east and west just after the barn. That right?"

Will nodded. Smiled. "Yes."

"Way I figure it, Will's house be on the low bluff over by the lake. Nice view of whole valley from there. Sarah has always loved the view from the plateau at the far end where the big river meets our river. Good site there to raise the family."

How does he know all this? Sarah thought.

"Pop, you been down to the city engineering offices?"

"No. Just how I see it is all."

Nothing wrong with your vision, Pop.

"Guess we'll get out of your hair, Dad."

"Be fine. Love you guys."

Sarah kissed his forehead. Boys waved.

Eli smirked.

Once the silence of the day hovered over E&E Estates, Ellie Ragsdale emerged beneath black surface of the boulder. She stood wagging a finger at her husband.

"Shame on you. Teasing with those kids like that."

"Sorry Ellie. Gotta have my fun somehow."

"That you did, Mister Ragsdale. That you did."

"We on schedule?" Eli asked.

"Mostly."

"*Mostly?* That doesn't sound good. This is serious stuff we're doing."

"Yes. It is."

"Anything I can do?"

"No. I think I can handle the next step. The painting and vacuuming was enough for you for now. Let me have some fun."

"That's a fact."

Twenty Six

Benjamin took a week off from his job to clear out of his studio on the Snohopi Slough and move in with Eli. Seemed odd to him, after all these years hardly speaking to his mother and father, to now be returning home to his same room in the house he grew up.

He was very surprised when he arrived.

Big bulldozer was already clearing driveways off the central drive towards the two home sites.

Big U-Haul van in the driveway. Eli, Will Keebler, Frank, and his two sons and daughter Cindy, all busy hauling Eli's furniture out the door.

"What's goin' on, Pop. Thought I was moving in!"

Is that Cindy Wallace?

"You are."

"But all the furniture. I mean, Pop, what are you doin'?"

Not seen her since high school.

"*Your* house, now. *Your* life. Best I move mine out."

"That Cindy Wallace helping you guys?" Benjamin said, distracted.

"Yes it is. You should say hello. Her husband died a couple years back. Works at the school district administration offices."

"Yeah. I will. So, where you gonna stay? We didn't discuss you moving out."

"Oh, I'm not moving out. Just cleaning out everything but my bedroom and some kitchen essentials. Leaves room for all your stuff."

"Pop! I don't have any . . . *stuff.*"

"I know. Good time for you to get some."

"Shit, Pop."

"Hey! Clean it up. Here comes Cindy."

She was average in most ways, much like Ellie Ragsdale. Nothing to set your bells ringing or make you hot and bothered.

Then again.

"So, Mister Benjamin Ragsdale. Been way too long." Cindy extended a hand.

Then again there was the smile.

Graceful stride.

Warm, firm grip. Voice like honey.

"Hi, Cindy. Yeah, it has. Pop told me about your husband. So sorry."

"Yes. Sad for me and our children. Grandchildren."

"Grandchildren? How many?"

"Six. Three and three."

Benjamin just nodded and smiled. Had he missed *all that*? Alone on the slough moaning, griping, pissed at the world for the hand he was dealt. An entire lifetime waltzed right on by him.

"Nice. Live around here?"

"Me or the grandchildren?"

"Um, both."

"Kids just north. Me? Live a mile from here just south. Lynch Hill Homes."

"Isn't that a 55 and older retirement place?"

"Yes. Sid and I had just moved in when he died. It's nice, but mostly much older folks. Too quiet. I grew up on a roaring farm with chores and all. Pace at Lynch Hill like driving slow in reverse."

Benjamin laughed.

"Sure like what you three are doing for Eli. Seems to agree with him. Good for you?"

"Yeah, I think so. All these years I've been . . . well, been out of the loop you might say."

She nodded, like she knew his life's history in every detail.

Eli approached. "You two remember each other?"

"Yes. We're just catching up some." Cindy said.

"Yeah, Pop. Yeah." Benjamin's voice trailed off as he continued to kick himself for the past forty years.

"Coffee some time?" Cindy asked.

Benjamin didn't respond.

"Ben? Coffee?"

"Um, sure. Love some."

Cindy laughed. "Where were you? I meant, would you like to meet for coffee sometime? Really catch up."

"Sorry. Yeah. Be nice. How's tomorrow? Nine. Small coffee shop downtown by the river."

"Eight's better."

"Eight."

"I'll be there. Now. How about helping us clear out *your* house for you?" She laughed.

He laughed with her.

Twenty Seven

Eli waved goodbye to all the Wallaces in various cars and trucks. Benjamin continued to shuffle his few belongings around inside the house. Eli limped through the dark to the barn. Body ached all over. Hit the switch filling the long, red building with warm fluorescent light. Pulled the sliding door aside. Ford turned over with little argument. Shortly, he pulled alongside the rock in the field.

Ellie.

He fumbled around in the dark. Sat on the loveseat.

Glow from the rock got his attention.

"Good day you had, Eli." Ellie said.

"*We* had."

"Yes, we are the old plotters, aren't we?"

"Hurt all over, El. Darn well worth it, though. Getting to spend time with Benjamin. And he seemed to enjoy seeing Cindy again."

"Oh, Eli. It's so grand watching you and Benjamin, all three really, getting to know each other better than ever."

"Just wish you didn't have to pass so we could."

"It's His plan, Eli. Not ours."

"I guess."

"And what about that Cindy? Eli, you miss so much. Benjamin nearly fell over when he saw her. Got all warm and fuzzy inside."

" 'Spose. And it looks like you made headway with City Hall, too." Eli laughed.

"Did at that. Dozer surprise you this morning?"

"Call it more like *scared shitless*."

"You did jump some."

They shared a momentary laugh.

"We on schedule, Ellie?" Eli said. His face crumpled a bit. Chin quivered.

"What's wrong?"

"Miss you something terrible."

"Oh, Eli. Miss you, too."

"Scared, some, too."

"Don't be. I'm *here* and it's incredible. Wonderful."

"Will I be able to hold you?"

"Yes, Eli. It's different than you think. I know what you've heard, read. So many well meaning people have told you what to expect when you get here. What the church teaches. *What you want to believe*. Thing is, no one knows for sure what this side is really like. Honestly, Eli, no one's ever been here who's come back to tell the tale."

"There's those near life experiences. You know, *going to that light* stuff they talk about."

"I know. And much of those are true. Those folks *did* have an experience of some sort. Touched death in a manner of speaking. It's sort of like how a legend grows. A story that's been added to so much, it's no longer the same event but one much grander. One that's been influenced by the media, movies, and others who have shared a similar event. Doesn't mean it didn't happen, but does leave a lot of questions."

"So, what *does* it mean?"

"Means you and I are getting into uncharted territory. What we're experiencing right this moment is a quantum leap from *going into the light* or *after death experience*. Eli, our story will *never* be told . . ."

"Ellie! The kids know!"

"... yes, they do. Um, but, Eli, we're getting ahead here. You'll need to be patient. Two weeks you'll be ninety years old. A milestone by any measure. We both know there will be a celebration and possibly for the first time in over forty years, all three of your children, *our* children, will be with you to sing Happy Birthday."

Sarcastic, "Wow! Can hardly wait. *Oh boy!* Big party and *no* Ellie. You know what that will be like?"

"Think I do. But you have to know in your heart I'm with you."

He mewled a little acknowledgment. Muddled in his own sorrow. Looked at her soft glow in the granite shadow across from him. Collected himself. "Yes. I guess if put into perspective, damn lucky, no, *blessed*, to still have you nearby."

"Amen to that." Ellie said softly.

"That's a fact."

Twenty Eight

With the house virtually empty after Eli's *stuff* was removed, Sarah planned his ninetieth birthday party at the old family home. With borrowed BBQ tables and chairs, she and her siblings and their wives set out a spread to end all spreads. Mostly Mexican food, plus burgers and hot dogs for the kids. Benjamin invited Cindy, whom he'd been seeing on and off since he first saw her again.

Rain moved the BBQ into the barn. Beer and wine followed.

The evening ended with a three layer chocolate cake, chocolate frosting and Mudslide ice cream. So much chocolate. Hardly Mexican.

Alone, surrounded by balloons and confetti, crepe spirals and a big looping sign reading *HAPPY BIRTHDAY*, Eli simply shrugged down in the loveseat brought in from the barn.

Felt Ellie's warmth.

Her touch.

"You okay, Pop?"

Benjamin's voice startled him. "Yes. Just thinking about your mother."

"I miss her, too, Pop. We all do."

"Know that."

"How?"

"What?"

"How do you miss her? I mean, what's it like losing someone you love so much?"

"Ben." He paused, choked back the tears. "Ben, it's not like anything you've ever experienced. It's down and dirty grief at first. You cry spontaneously. Cry so hard you almost embarrass yourself. Then there's the gaps."

"Gaps?"

"Yeah, those little places where she *should* be. Still in bed waiting for stove heat to reach her. Kitchen table sippin' morning coffee. Bed next to me. Standing on the PTO when I worked the field. Sitting in the seat next to me at church. Holding my hand on walks to the river. Her empty, worn spot at the base of the fir."

"But she *is* out there. The rock."

Eli nodded. *She was out there.*

"Yeah, she is out there. Gotta love that for sure."

"Yeah. Very cool."

Standing, Eli put a weathered hand on Benjamin's shoulder. "Cindy. Anything there?"

"Some. Not sure. She's fun to talk to. We have so much in common. I think she's kinda interested in me."

"Lord help us!"

"Pop!"

"Good night, son. Glad you're here. I love you very much."

"Me, too, Pop. Me, too."

There was an abrupt, awkward hug. Eli kissed Benjamin's neck. Trundled off to his room at the back of the house.

Benjamin watched Eli disappear down the hall.

Rubbed his neck.

Twenty Nine

Four months, give or take a few days, both Sarah's and Will's homes were completed. Two months ahead of schedule. Just before the first serious October winds and rain. Trucks and vans and contractors came and went daily during the last days of construction.

Benjamin's remodeling was complete. New furniture, window coverings, walls painted with a blessing from Cindy.

Eli sat on the loveseat laughing and enjoying each moment with Ellie.

Time to time one of the three siblings would have to explain the old man in the lean-to by the boulder, but in time most barely noticed it.

"We done, Ellie?"

"Almost."

"What's left?"

"The hard part." Ellie said.

"For whom?"

"All of us."

"No other way?" He asked.

"No."

"When?"

"Now."

"Crap."

"Yes, Eli. That's a fact."

Thirty

Eli bumped along on his Ford 9N. Smoke billowed behind. Overcast sky a flat gray panel as if a painted ceiling. Odor of cooking meat floated on the wind. Distant BBQ. Eli curled the tractor into the barn. Engine coughed off. He sat in the dark clutching the steering wheel. Fingering the cracked shift knob. Ran a rough hand over the tire tread. Took in the moldy smell of the barn he built so long ago.

Sure glad we didn't bury Buckshot in here.

Pulled the door closed. Stumbled some into the house.

Sarah greeted him.

"Dad. You look beat. Beer?"

"Glass of Merlot would be good."

"Coming up."

Eli showered. Shaved. Clean t-shirt. Sweatshirt didn't smell. Put it on.

Took the glass of wine. Sat.

"To you three." He toasted.

Before him, a sight he thought he'd never see. His and Ellie's three children together, smiling and laughing. They lifted their glasses.

Will sat. "So, Dad. What's up that you needed to see us?"

Not so sure I can do this, Ellie.

Yes. You can.

Eli sipped his wine looking through the glass at three of the finest people he'd ever known. Set the glass down.

"Gotta be goin'."

"Trip?"

"*Finally!* You're taking a vacation."

"Where to, Pop?"

"Be with your mother."

Sarah dropped her wineglass on the new, tile floor. Burst to tears. She understood.

Both brothers jumped at the crashing glass. Will dropped to his knees, shoulders shuttering up and down. As usual, Benjamin probed for more."

"What's that mean, *be with your mother?* Mom's . . .oh, shit!"

Eli sat. Shaking.

This was going to be hard.

Tears streamed from each eye as he watched his three adult children collate what he'd said with what they knew or thought. It was gut-wrenching.

Hang in there, Eli. Remember why we did this.

He did.

Mustering what strength he had, "Fill your glasses and follow me to the rock." Eli said, standing, walking through the kitchen.

Outside Mother Nature was wreaking havoc. Rain pelted the metal barn into a roar. Puddles splashed, wind howled. Eli stepped out the backdoor to the small patio and waited.

Three joined him. Touching him. Holding onto him.

Not another word was spoken, but the dry, warm, windless trip to the rock did not go unnoticed.

"Ellie. We're here."

She emerged immediately. "See that."

"Best you do this."

"I will."

"Hi Mom." Benjamin said. Others waved.

"Hi Benjamin. Sarah. Will. This will be brief. Know you will understand."

"Already a bit hard to get, Mom." Will said through whimpers.

Eli put an arm around the much taller man.

"We know this has been trying, if not downright weird. Not everyone gets to talk to their deceased mother who mysteriously shows up as a reflection in a rock."

Abruptly, Ellie Elizabeth Ragsdale stepped from the rock.

Soundless. Fluid.

Ghostlike.

Eli caught Sarah before she hit the ground. Brothers took her.

Ellie took Sarah into her arms. "Sorry, Sarah."

Benjamin shook his head, "Why?"

"Why what?" Eli asked.

"Why all this? It's plain weird. Why us? Why the Ragsdales?"

Holding onto Sarah, Ellie answered. "I suppose *why not* is really the question."

She paused, chuckled to herself. "Answer's long and convoluted. Yet simple. But I'll try. Run a few thoughts for you to consider. First, this is *not* the first time this has happened. Happens every day. You just don't hear about it."

"Happens every day? In a rock?"

Ellie laughed. "Heavens no. This big black rock was my choice. I thought it was beautiful and, well, I've always had a thing for river rocks."

"So . . .?"

"What do others do?" Ellie cut in.

Sarah nodded.

"Water. Mirrors are terrific. Trees. The wind. Know of one gentleman who appeared from a free standing wood stove. Don't ask. People get to choose what they want. Like Hal and Becky Struther, next door. She arrived in the yard before Hal as a deer. And no one ever knew about these occurrences when all was said and done."

"Why's that?" Will sniffled. "This would be world shaking news."

"Let me finish. Like I said, it happened to Struthers next door in 1998. Remember the McGees? 1992. And the Barstows from the YMCA. 2002. Happens all the time. All around you. Fact is, happens to every couple who loves so deep like me and your father."

"Mom!"

"I know. Lot to chew on, but it's so."

"But . . ."

"But why don't we hear more about this?

All three nodded.

Ellie looked at Eli. Smiled. He nodded to her.

"Because after your father . . ."

Ellie choked back her words. Struggled. Eli took her hands. The three children huddled around holding. Crying.

" . . . after your father joins me, it will all disappear."

"You mean Pop?"

She shook her head. "The memory."

"Of you two?"

Ellie let go of Sarah. Stepped back. "Of course not. But all the events related to seeing me in the boulder will be erased. Never happened. It's why you never hear about it. Smoke on the wind. Oh, life will go on, but this little family moment will evaporate."

"*Shit!*"

"I suppose."

"*Damn!*"

"That's a fact."

"*When?*"

"Now."

"Oh, no. Mom. Dad. We can't be done. No. No. No." Sarah sank into her father's arms. Held tight. The boys clung to Ellie.

Sarah screamed. "Not now. We're all together."

Yes. Finally. Ellie purred.

She held up a hand. "We know. We know. *That* was the plan."

"The plan?"

Behind Ellie, like a phone ringing, the rock emitted a low-grade hum. Ellie gently pulled away from the boys. Eli released Sarah watching Ellie.

Ellie nodded. Returned to her rock.

"What now?" Will asked soberly.

"I must leave you." Ellie said.

"Forever."

She nodded. "Always be a heart thought away."

Sarah sobbed. Hugged Will.

"And Pop?" Benjamin asked.

"He'll be fine." She said and disappeared into the black stone.

"*Fine?* He'll be fine? What's that mean?"

"Means I'll be fine. Back to the house. Gettin' cold." Eli said.

They all at once noticed the slanting rain. Numbing chill. Ran to the house best they could.

Inside, Eli filled their wine again. Hugged each one separately. Lifted his glass.

"To your mother. God rest her gorgeous soul to eternity."

Thirty One

They buried Eli Ragsdale's ashes in a simple plot next to his wife of forever. Her ashes were not there. No one knew that for sure.

Except Eli.

Graves huddled beneath a fir tree in the Mountain View Cemetery. Both had a carved headstone.

Kind words hung in the air. Hugs and tears spread around the grounds and the hundred or so faithful friends and family moved about sharing stories of Eli.

And his eternal love for Ellie.

Sarah held tight to her brothers' hands, one on each side as they hovered between the two graves. Eli's modest coffin resting so forever far beneath the surface.

"Place won't be the same. Gonna miss that old guy." Benjamin said.

"Yeah. Me, too." Sarah said.

Will nodded.

They were all cried out.

"Dad leave each of you a note like this?" Asked Will holding up a small, white envelope.

"Yes." They both said.

"Envelope says to open it now. Here over his grave."

"Not mine. Says to open it at the house." Benjamin said waving his envelope.

"Mine says to open it tomorrow morning in the barn." Sarah said.

"That's silly. Let's open them all right now."

"No, Ben! Let's do it the way he wanted."

"Crap. So, open yours, Will."

He did.

"It's short. All it says is he's proud of us. Loves how we're a family again. No matter how much Benjamin whines, do what the other envelopes say."

They exchanged glances and broke out laughing.

Next morning, they stood quietly together in the farmhouse kitchen. Each clung to a cup of hot coffee. Benjamin fumbled with his envelope. He read it. "Says he's proud how we handled dividing up the property, building our homes and such. Again, says glad we're together as siblings. Loves us. That's it."

"To the barn." Sarah said.

Outside, another cool, gray fall day. Winter on the horizon. They could see the morning lights in Sarah's new house. Will's just out of sight, but chimney smoke curled into the sky above where the house sat. They walked to the barn, each eying the mysterious black rock resting ominously out in the field.

"What we gonna do about that boulder, anyway? Sure messes up the field for farming." Benjamin said.

Will nodded his agreement. "Still wonder where it came from. Sure had dad stumped."

"Looks damn lonely out there." Sarah said.

She stopped a moment, staring at the rock. Shook her head.

Inside, she flipped on the overhead lights. Eli's tractor sat looking at them. Skidder still hooked to the PTO. Sarah jumped to the tractor's metal seat. Sat and wrestled with the envelope.

She read the note. Held it up waving the note in one hand, torn envelope in the other. "Says to go out to the rock."

"That's it?"

"Yes."

"Shit."

"Okay."

They walked and chatted. Heads down against the wind and slanting rain. Careful to step over puddles and mud. Sarah was the first to look up at the rock.

"My God!"

Boys lifted their heads.

A second boulder, equally as large, rested at a comfortable angle next to the first.

Touching.

It, too, embedded in the ground, was a deep, shiny black. Both pointing directly at the fir tree where Eli and Ellie Ragsdale once cuddled.

Forehead to forehead.

Sipping coffee.

Watching for salmon.

That's a fact.

End

Made in the USA
Charleston, SC
26 November 2011